From the diary of Finola Elliott

Travis Clayton says he's "a simple country boy," but there isn't anything simple about him! In that cowboy hat of his, the man is six feet four inches of pure sex appeal. He can heat up a fall night faster than a blast furnace.

Being in his presence confounds me. I'm Fin Elliott, editor in chief of one of the world's biggest fashion magazines. A fearless executive who can face any challenge set before me and come out the victor. Why, then, can't I face my feelings for Travis?

It's the baby. My hormones have me tied up in knots. In two months Patrick's ridiculous contest for control of the Elliott publishing empire ends and I can taste victory. I can't wait to see his grizzled face when I take over as CEO. But how can I work twenty hours a day when I'll be a new mother? What do I do about the baby?

And, God help me, what do I do about Travis?

Is he the one challenge I can't meet?

Dear Reader,

I think at one time or another in life, we've all wished for a second chance to do something or wondered what choices we would have made if we could go back in time and do certain things differently. But other than a mulligan in golf or a "do over" in a neighborhood ball game, there are very few times when we're given that opportunity.

That's why I was thrilled when I was invited to write a book for THE ELLIOTTS and learned that my story was all about second chances. I really enjoyed writing the journey Fin and Travis take as they find the courage to reach for their second chance at parenthood, family relationships and love. It is my fervent hope that you enjoy it, too.

All the best,

Kathie DeNosky

KATHIE DeNOSKY

THE EXPECTANT EXECUTIVE

Published by Silhouette Books
America's Publisher of Contemporary Romance

This book is dedicated to the authors of THE ELLIOTTS.
You gals are awesome and it was a privilege and
an honor to work with you.

Special thanks and acknowledgment are given to
Kathie DeNosky for her contribution
to THE ELLIOTTS miniseries.

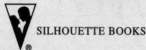 SILHOUETTE BOOKS

ISBN-13: 978-0-373-76759-5
ISBN-10: 0-373-76759-5

THE EXPECTANT EXECUTIVE

Printed in U.S.A.

KATHIE DeNOSKY

lives in her native southern Illinois with her husband and one very spoiled Jack Russell terrier. She writes highly sensual stories with a generous amount of humor. Kathie's books have appeared on the Waldenbooks bestseller list and received the Write Touch Readers' Award from *WisRWA* and the National Readers' Choice Award. She enjoys going to rodeos, traveling to research settings for her books and listening to country music. Readers may contact Kathie at P.O. Box 2064, Herrin, Illinois 62948-5264 or e-mail her at kathie@kathiedenosky.com.

THE ELLIOTTS

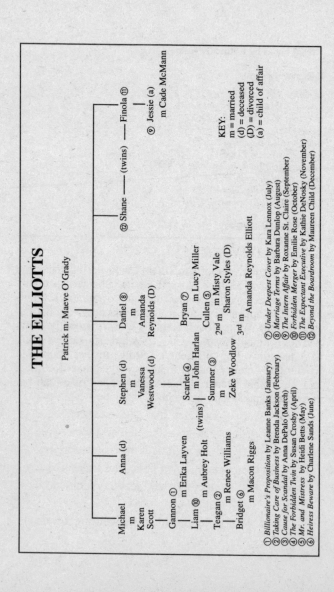

Patrick. m. Maeve O'Grady

Michael m Karen Scott

Anna (d)

Stephen (d) m Vanessa Westwood (d)

Daniel ⑧ m Amanda Reynolds (D)

㉒ Shane ——— Finola ⑪

Gannon ①
m Erika Layven

Liam ⑩
(twins)
m Aubrey Holt

Scarlet ④
m John Harlan

Bryan ⑦
m Lucy Miller

⑨ Jessie (a)
m Cade McMann

Teagan ②
m Renee Williams

Summer ③
m Zeke Woodlow

Cullen ⑤
2ⁿᵈ m Misty Vale
m Sharon Styles (D)

Bridget ⑥
m Macon Riggs

3ʳᵈ m Amanda Reynolds Elliott

KEY:
m = married
(d) = deceased
(D) = divorced
(a) = child of affair

① Billionaire's Proposition by Leanne Banks (January)
② Taking Care of Business by Brenda Jackson (February)
③ Cause for Scandal by Anna DePalo (March)
④ The Forbidden Twin by Susan Crosby (April)
⑤ Mr. and Mistress by Heidi Betts (May)
⑥ Heiress Beware by Charlene Sands (June)
⑦ Under Deepest Cover by Kara Lennox (July)
⑧ Marriage Terms by Barbara Dunlop (August)
⑨ The Intern Affair by Roxanne St. Claire (September)
⑩ The Forbidden Merger by Emilie Rose (October)
⑪ The Expectant Executive by Kathie DeNosky (November)
⑫ Beyond the Boardroom by Maureen Child (December)

One

"I can't believe it's already the first of November," Finola Elliott muttered as she scanned the entries in her electronic planner.

There were only two months left before Patrick, founder and CEO of Elliott Publication Holdings and patriarch of the Long Island Elliott clan, retired and named one of his four children his successor to the magazine empire he'd built over the years. And Fin had every intention of being the indisputable winner of the competition he'd set up to decide who would best fill that role.

She'd spent her entire adult life working toward

taking over EPH, and even though her two brothers and one nephew were all equally qualified for the position, Patrick—she hadn't referred to him as her father in years—owed her the job and so much more. But when he reviewed the growth and profit margins of *The Buzz*, *Snap*, *Pulse* and *Charisma* magazines, Fin wanted there to be no mistaking that her "baby," *Charisma*, had outdistanced the others, hands down.

At the end of the second quarter, her fashion magazine had been in the lead. Unfortunately, in the past couple of months her twin brother, Shane, had pulled ahead with his show business publication, *The Buzz*. But Fin wasn't overly concerned. Everything was back on track and going her way again.

Smiling fondly, she glanced at the newly framed picture on her desk and the reason her attention had been diverted from the objective. She'd discovered that her intern, Jessica Clayton, was the baby girl Patrick had forced Fin to give up for adoption twenty-three years ago, and she and her daughter had been making up for lost time. Jessie was a wonderful young woman and they'd become quite close over the past couple of months. In fact, Fin had even accompanied Jessie to the Silver Moon Ranch in Colorado, to meet Jessie's adoptive father and see where she'd grown up.

But now that Jessie and Cade McMann, Fin's right-hand man at *Charisma*, were busy with the final preparations for their wedding later in the month, Fin needed to get back on track and regain her focus. She hid a yawn behind her hand. She just wished she wasn't so darned tired all the time.

As she switched to the month of October to review her notes on the magazine's growth projections for November, goose bumps skittered over her skin and a little chill streaked up her spine.

Something was missing. Where was the personal notation she made every month marking the start of her cycle?

Switching back to her entry in September, her heart slammed to a stop, then pounded hard against her ribs. She hadn't had a period in almost six weeks?

"That can't be right."

Surely she'd just forgotten to record the date for October. But as she thought back, she couldn't remember having had a period since well before accompanying Jessie to Colorado.

Stunned, Fin sat back in her high-backed leather chair and stared out the plateglass windows at the Manhattan skyline. The only other time in her life that she'd skipped her cycle had been at the age of fifteen when she'd gotten pregnant after her one night of passion with her sixteen-year-old boyfriend, Sebastian Deveraux. But there was absolutely no way she could be pregnant this time.

She almost laughed. For that to even be a remote possibility, she'd have to have a love life. And she didn't. She couldn't even remember the last time she'd been out with a man when the evening hadn't been business-related—either courting a potential advertising client or entertaining one of the many designers featuring his or her new line in *Charisma*.

Her social life had taken, and probably always would take, a backseat to the magazine that had become her obsession over the years. But a sudden thought caused her to catch her breath. There had been that one night at the party Travis Clayton, Jessie's adoptive father, had thrown in honor of Jessie and Cade's engagement.

Fin's cheeks heated at the thought of just what had taken place when she and Travis had gone into that charming old barn of his to check on a mare and her new foal. What had started out to be an innocent hug to express how grateful she was that Travis and his late wife, Lauren, had done such a wonderful job of raising Jessie, had turned into a passionate encounter that still left Fin feeling breathlessly weak. There had only been one other time in her life that she'd allowed herself to lose control and throw caution to the wind like that. The night she'd conceived Jessie.

She thoughtfully nibbled on her lower lip. She couldn't possibly have gotten pregnant from that one stolen moment with Travis, could she?

Shaking her head, she dismissed the idea outright. It might be possible, but it was most definitely improbable. She'd read somewhere that the closer a woman got to forty, the longer it sometimes took to become pregnant. And at thirty-eight, she was closing in on forty faster than she cared to admit.

Besides, fate couldn't possibly be that cruel. She'd conceived Jessie the night she'd lost her virginity to Sebastian. Surely the odds of her becoming pregnant again after making love with a man one time had to be astronomical.

No, missing her period had to be an indication that something else was wrong.

Swiveling her chair around, she reached for the phone to make an appointment with her gynecologist, but gasped at the unexpected sight of Travis Clayton leaning one broad shoulder against her doorframe.

"I know I'm not the best-looking thing to come down the pike, but I wasn't aware that I'd started scaring the hell out of pretty women and little kids," he said, his deep voice filled with humor.

The teasing light in his sinfully blue eyes sent a delicious warmth coursing throughout her body. If she'd ever seen a man as ruggedly handsome as Jessie's adoptive father, Fin couldn't remember when. Looking much younger than his forty-nine years, he was the epitome of the modern western man from the top of his wide-brimmed black cowboy hat all the way to his big-booted feet. Wearing a pair of soft-looking, well-worn jeans, chambray shirt and a western-cut sports jacket that emphasized the breadth of his impossibly wide shoulders, he could easily be one of the male models in an advertisement for men's cologne.

"Travis, it's good to see you again. I don't remember Jessie mentioning that you would be visiting this week." Rising to her feet, Fin walked around the desk to greet him. "Please, come in and sit down."

Giving her a smile that caused her toes to curl inside her Italian designer heels, he straightened to his full height and crossed the room with the confidence and grace of a man quite comfortable with who he was and what he was about. "When I talked to Jess the other day, she sounded a little hassled from all this wedding stuff, so I decided to surprise her," he said, settling into one of the chairs in front of Fin's desk.

"A little paternal support never hurts," she agreed, wondering what it would be like to have a father who was sensitive to his child's emotional needs. Patrick's approach to childrearing had been nothing short of dictatorial and he could have cared less how his issued orders affected his offspring's emotions—in particular, hers.

"How have you been, Fin?" Travis asked when she sat down in the chair beside him.

The warmth and genuine interest in his smooth baritone sent a little shiver up her spine. "Fine. And yourself?"

He shrugged. "Can't complain." Looking around her office, his curious gaze seemed to zero in on a stack of ad proofs on her desk. "When I asked Jess how you've been getting on, she said you're working like crazy to win this contest your dad set up."

Her stomach did a funny little flip at the thought that he'd been asking Jessie about her. "The competition and helping with Jessie and Cade's wedding arrangements have been keeping me pretty busy."

"I'll bet it has." He chuckled. "All this wedding hoopla makes me kind of glad I'm stuck off in no-man's-land until it's time to walk her down the aisle. Jess said all I have to do is go for the final fitting on my tux while I'm in town and that suits me just fine."

He wasn't fooling Fin for a minute. Travis and Jessie had a wonderful father-daughter relationship and he had to be feeling a little left out for him to fly all the way from Colorado.

"This is pretty tough for you, isn't it?"

He started to shake his head, then looking a bit sheepish, he grinned. "It shows that much, does it? I thought I was doing a pretty fair job of hiding it, but I guess I was wrong."

Fin nodded sympathetically. "I'm sure it's a difficult transition to suddenly be relegated to the number-two man in your daughter's life when you've always been number one."

"I can't believe she's old enough to get married," he said, removing his hat to run his hand through his thick dark blond hair. Replacing his hat, his expression turned wistful. "It seems like just yesterday I was kissing her skinned elbows and teaching her how to print her name for kindergarten."

A little pang of envy gripped Fin's heart. She'd been cheated out of so much when Patrick had forced her to give her baby daughter up for adoption.

They sat in silence for several long moments before Travis spoke again. "I know this is short notice, but I stopped by to ask if you'd like to join Jessie and me for supper this evening. We'll be meeting at some place she called the Lemon Grill."

He grinned. "If the name is any indication, it sounds like a place a man could get a decent steak."

Fin smiled. "I'm sure you can. It's a charming little bistro with excellent food."

"Then you'll join us?"

She should decline the invitation outright. She and Travis had absolutely nothing in common beyond their love for Jessie. But for reasons beyond her comprehension, Fin was drawn to Travis and had been since the moment they met.

"I don't want to intrude on your time with your daughter," she hedged.

He shook his head. "She's your daughter, too. Besides, I wouldn't have asked if I hadn't wanted you to join us. And I'm sure you want to spend as much time with her as you can now that you two have found each other."

Her heart filled with emotion when he referred to Jessie as her daughter, too. "You're sure you don't mind?"

When he took her hand in his much larger one, a tingling thrill streaked up Fin's arm at the feel of his work-callused palm against her much softer skin. "I'm positive." The warmth in his incredibly blue eyes assured her that he did indeed want her to have dinner with them. "What man wouldn't want to be out with the two best-looking women in this whole damned town?"

The truth was, spending the evening with Travis and Jessie was far more appealing than sitting alone in her too-big apartment eating take out and going over spread sheets filled with *Charisma*'s growth projections and profit margins. Surely one more night of putting off the task wasn't going to hurt her chances of winning the competition for EPH.

"Wh-what time should I meet you at the bistro?" Why did she suddenly feel like a teenage girl being asked to the homecoming dance by the best-looking, most popular boy in school?

"Eight." Still holding her hand, he rose to his feet, then pulled her up to stand beside him. "I guess I'd better let you get back to work if you're going to win your dad's contest."

"I suppose that would be a good idea." Why didn't she sound as resolute about it as she would have before he appeared at her door?

He leaned forward to press a soft kiss to her forehead. "Then I'll see you this evening, Fin."

Her skin tingled where his lips had been and before she could find her voice, Travis touched the wide brim of his cowboy hat in a gallant gesture and turned to walk away.

As she watched him disappear into the outer

office, she felt the need to fan herself. Dear God, the man was six feet four inches of pure sex appeal and could heat up a room faster than a blast furnace. His kiss had only been meant as a friendly gesture, but her heart had skipped several beats at the touch of his lips to her suddenly overly sensitive skin.

"Was that the model for Calvin Klein's new cowboy cologne?" Chloe Davenport asked, entering Fin's office. She glanced over her shoulder at Travis. "If so, could I sign up to be his cowgirl?"

Fin laughed at her executive assistant. "No. That's Travis Clayton, Jessie's father."

"You're kidding." Fin watched the young woman take another lingering glance before closing the office door. "He's the real deal, isn't he?"

"If by that you mean that he's a working cowboy, then yes, he's the real thing."

Chloe sighed wistfully. "If they grow them like that in Colorado, I just might have to head that way sometime."

Fin laughed. "And leave that cute little apartment you have in Chelsea?"

"Ooh, that would be a problem. I finally have it decorated just the way I want it," Chloe said, handing Fin the latest accounting reports. "I suppose

I'll just have to stay in New York and content myself with finding an urban cowboy."

Fin nodded, distracted by the report. "What's the latest word around EPH? Anything going on with the other magazines that I should know about?"

The young woman shook her head. "Not that I've heard. You and Shane are still the top contenders for CEO. *The Buzz*'s growth and profit margin is slightly better than *Charisma*'s, but the consensus in accounting is that *Charisma* could still come out the winner."

"G-good." Suddenly feeling a bit dizzy, Fin walked around her desk to sit in her high-backed chair. She definitely needed to see a doctor.

"Fin, are you okay?" Chloe asked, her pretty young face marred with concern.

Nodding, Fin gave her a weak smile. "I'm just tired, that's all."

"I'm worried about you, Fin. You've been working way too hard." Chloe frowned. "You've always been driven, but these past ten months you've made workaholics look like total slackers."

"I'll be fine, Chloe."

Her assistant looked doubtful. "Are you sure about that?"

Smiling, Fin nodded as she handed the report back to her assistant. "Now, go give these to Cade and tell him that I want to meet with him first thing in the morning to go over these figures."

"Anything else?"

Fin checked the clock. "No, I have a few phone calls to make, then I think I'm going to take off the rest of the day."

Chloe looked thunderstruck. "You're kidding. You never leave before eight or nine in the evening and more times than I care to count, I've found you sleeping on your couch when I arrive for work. Are you sure you're feeling all right? Should I call someone?"

"No, you don't need to call anyone." Smiling, Fin hid a yawn behind her hand. "I have a dinner engagement and I think I need a short nap to make it through the evening. Otherwise, I might fall asleep between the appetizer and the main course."

"That wouldn't be good for business," Chloe agreed, shaking her head as she walked to the door.

Fin didn't bother to correct her assistant as the young woman quietly closed the door behind her. Dinner this evening had nothing whatsoever to do with business and everything to do with pleasure. Her only concern was deciding which she was anticipating more—the pleasure of spending time with her newfound daughter or her daughter's adoptive father.

* * *

Travis felt like a fish out of water. The concrete and steel of New York City was a far cry from the wide open spaces he was used to and the Lemon Grill was to hell and gone from the little diner he sometimes frequented when he drove over to Winchester County for the stock auctions. Here he sat in an upscale café in the middle of Manhattan with a prissy little waiter sporting a pencil-thin mustache and slicked-back hair, hovering around him like a bumblebee over a patch of new spring clover.

"My name is Henri. It will be my pleasure to be your server this evening." The too-polished character smiled, showing off a set of unnaturally white teeth. "Would the gentleman like something to drink while he's waiting on his dinner partners?"

Travis frowned. The little guy sure spouted out a lot of words to ask a simple question. He was more used to being asked straight up what he wanted to drink instead of being referred to like he was some sort of third wheel.

"I'll take a beer."

"Would the gentleman like a domestic brand or imported?"

Unable to resist teasing the pretentious little man, Travis grinned. "I can't say what the gentleman would like, but I'll take domestic." As Henri started to leave the table, Travis added the name of a beer brewed exclusively in the Rocky Mountains.

"I'm sorry, sir. We don't carry that particular brand," Henri said, his apology as fake as his cap-toothed smile. Rattling off a list of the beer the restaurant had available, he asked, "Would the gentleman like to choose one of those?"

"Surprise me."

"Very well, sir."

As the waiter hurried away to get his drink, Travis spotted Fin entering the restaurant. She briefly spoke to the hostess, then when she headed his way, he couldn't help but marvel at what a beauty she was. With her straight, dark auburn hair stylishly brushing her shoulders, and looking like a model in her black form-fitting dress, she looked far too young to be the mother of his twenty-three-year-old daughter.

Standing when she approached, he thought his heart would jump right out of his chest when her perfect coral lips turned up in a warm smile. "I hope I'm not too late. The crosstown traffic was particularly heavy this evening."

"You drove?" He held the chair for her while she seated herself at the small table. "I remember Jessie telling me that you'd never learned to drive."

Fin's delightful laughter caused an unexpected

heat to settle in the pit of his belly as he sat back down. "Guilty as charged. I've never even been behind the wheel of a car."

"You're kidding, right?" Hell, he'd been driving around the ranch in either a truck or on a tractor since he was ten years old and he'd taught Jessie to drive when she was twelve. "You've never—"

"No. When my brothers and I lived at home, we always had drivers to take us wherever we wanted to go. Then, after I moved from the Hamptons into my Manhattan apartment, there was no need to drive. Everything I need is so close, I walk a lot. And when where I want to go is too far to walk, I use the corporate limo or take a taxi." Her eyes twinkled wistfully as she added, "But I've always thought it might be fun to learn how to drive a car."

"The next time you visit the Silver Moon, I'll teach you," he said, unable to wipe what he was sure had to be a sappy grin from his face.

Her eyes held a warmth that stole his breath. "I'd like that, Travis. Thank you."

The thought of Fin coming back to his ranch for a visit had his heart pounding like the bass drum in a marching band. But it was the slight blush on her porcelain cheeks and the warmth in her pretty green eyes that caused the region south of his belt buckle to tighten. She remembered what happened between them when she visited his ranch last month, the same as he did.

"Would the lady like something to drink before ordering dinner?" Henri asked, returning to their table with Travis's beer.

For reasons Travis didn't want to dwell on, the man's appreciative grin when he looked at Fin irritated the hell out of Travis.

"Just some water with a slice of lemon, please," Fin answered the prissy little guy. As he moved away to take care of her request, she asked, "Where's Jessie? I was sure she'd be here by now."

Travis shook his head. "I don't know. She said something about going with Cade to pick up airline tickets for their honeymoon after they got off work. But that was a good three hours ago. Surely it doesn't take that long to…"

His voice trailed off when he felt Fin's soft, delicate hand touch his. "I'm sure she's fine, Travis. I overheard her and Cade talking about a stop at the jeweler's to pick up gifts for their bridesmaids and groomsmen. Maybe it took longer than they had anticipated."

As he sat there trying to force words around the cotton suddenly coating his throat, Henri placed a glass of water on the table in front of Fin. "Sir, you have a phone call. If you'll follow me, you may take the call at the hostess's desk."

When Travis glanced at Fin, she smiled. "It's probably Jessie telling you that she's held up in traffic."

"I hope you're right." He briefly wondered why his daughter hadn't called his cell phone, until he remembered that he'd turned it off when he entered the restaurant.

Excusing himself, Travis quickly made his way to the front of the restaurant. Even though Jess had been living in New York City for the better part of a year, it still made him nervous to think of his little girl on the mean streets of a big city. He'd relaxed a little after meeting her fiancé, Cade McMann, and being assured that the man had every intention of keeping her safe and making her happy. But if something had happened to her, Travis would have Cade's head on a silver platter for not taking better care of her.

When the hostess handed him the phone, he was relieved to hear his precious daughter on the other end of the line. "Hi, Daddy."

"Where are you, angel? Are you all right?"

"I'm fine, but I'm afraid I won't be able to meet you and Fin for dinner this evening." There was a short silence before she added, "I've, um, got a headache and I think I'll turn in early. You don't mind having dinner alone with Fin, do you?"

"Of course not, princess." Travis glanced over at the beautiful woman waiting patiently at his table. He'd have to be as crazy as a horse after it got into a patch of locoweed to mind spending time with her.

"Good. I'm sure you'll both enjoy yourselves. The Lemon Grill has great food." Jessie's voice was a little too enthusiastic and she didn't sound the least bit under the weather. "Please give Fin my apologies and tell her that I'll see her at the office tomorrow morning."

"I'll do that, angel." She wasn't fooling him for a minute. Jess had been after him for the past couple of years to get out more and revitalize his social life, as she put it. And unless he missed his guess, his little girl was trying to play matchmaker between him and her biological mother.

"Oh, don't forget, Daddy. We're supposed to meet for lunch tomorrow, then go to the men's store to have you fitted for your tux."

"You're still going to make me wear that monkey suit, are you?"

"You'll be the best looking monkey at the wedding," she said, laughing. "I love you, Daddy. See you tomorrow."

"I love you too, Jess."

Handing the cordless phone back to the hostess, Travis walked over to the table where Fin sat waiting for him. "Looks like it's just the two of us for supper tonight," he said, settling into his chair.

She gave him a questioning look. "Jessie isn't coming?"

"Nope." He shook his head. "She said she has a headache and intends to go to bed early."

"Since your other dinner partner won't be joining you, would you care to order now?" Henri asked, suddenly appearing at Travis's elbow. The man had obviously been eavesdropping on their conversation.

Tired of the waiter's obtrusive presence, Travis gave him a look that had the little man quickly fading into the background without another word. "What do you say we go somewhere we can talk without old Ornery over there hanging on our every word?"

Fin looked puzzled. "Ornery?"

"Henri. Ornery." Travis grinned. "Same difference."

She gave him a smile that did strange things to his insides. "I think I know of a place where we can talk uninterrupted."

"Sounds good to me." Raising his hand, he motioned to Henri.

The little waiter was at Travis's side almost immediately. "Would the lady and gentleman like to order now?"

Fin spoke up before Travis had a chance. "No, we've changed our minds and won't be dining with you this evening."

Leaving Henri to hover over someone else, when they stepped out onto the street, Travis put his arm around Fin to shelter her from the chilly November wind. Her slender body pressed to his side sent his blood pressure up a good fifty points and brought back memories of the last time he'd held her close. His body tightened predictably and he felt as if his jeans had shrunk a size or two in the stride.

"What's the name of this restaurant where the waiters leave the customers alone?" he asked when he finally got his voice to work.

"Chez Fin Elliott."

His heart stuttered and he had to remind himself to breathe. "We're going to your place?"

Nodding, she smiled. "If you don't mind missing out on your steak, I thought we could go back to my apartment, order in some Chinese and talk without having someone else hanging on our every word."

He wasn't wild about egg rolls and chop suey, but he'd have to be a damned fool to pass up spending the evening alone with one of the most beautiful women he'd ever had the privilege to lay eyes on.

Before she had a chance to change her mind, Travis raised his arm and waved at an approaching yellow car. "Taxi!"

Two

As Fin phoned in a delivery order to her favorite Chinese restaurant, she watched Travis glance around her cavernous Upper East Side apartment and couldn't help but wonder what he thought of her personal space. Obscenely spacious for one person, it was a study in chrome and glass, black and white, and light-years away from his warmly decorated home in Colorado.

When she'd visited the Silver Moon Ranch, she'd found the house to be roomy and pleasantly cluttered, but it was also welcoming, cozy and everything her apartment wasn't. While Travis's rustic home had the unmistakable look and feel of being lived in and enjoyed—of love and family—her apartment appeared to be stark, cold and uninhabited in comparison.

Of course, that might have something to do with the fact that she was never there for more than a few hours at a time, nor had she made the effort to add anything to reflect her own personality after the interior designer had finished decorating the place. The really sad thing was, that had been several years ago and she still had no more interest in personalizing the place than she had the day she'd moved in.

"Mr. Chang assured me the food will be here in less than fifteen minutes," she said as she ended the phone call. "Would you like something to drink while we wait? I think I have a bottle of wine in the refrigerator or I could make a pot of coffee or tea."

"A cup of coffee would be nice."

When he turned to face her, Travis's smile sent a wave of goose bumps shimmering over her skin and a delicious little shiver straight up her spine. He was, without a doubt, one of the sexiest men she'd ever met. And she seriously doubted that he had the slightest clue of how handsome he was or the tantalizing effect he had on women.

Suddenly needing to put a little space between them before she made a complete fool of herself, Fin started toward the kitchen. He was her daughter's adoptive father, the man who had, along with his late wife, raised the little girl Fin had been forced to give up for adoption all those years ago. The last thing she needed to do was complicate the fledgling relationship she had with Jessica by lusting after Travis. Come to think of it, it was totally out of character for her to be lusting after anyone.

"I'll start the coffeemaker."

"Need help?"

She stopped in her tracks, then slowly turned to face him. Even as he stood all the way across the living room, his presence made the space feel decidedly smaller than it had when they'd first walked through the door. She could only imagine how minuscule the kitchen would seem with him in much closer proximity. Besides, having him join her would defeat the purpose of her much needed escape.

"No." To soften her hasty reply, she smiled. "By no stretch of the imagination am I domestic, but I think I can manage a pot of coffee without too much trouble." Waving her hand toward the white velour sofa, she added, "I'll only be a few minutes. Why don't you make yourself comfortable?"

"I think I'll do that." His grin sent a wave of heat from the top of her head to the soles of her feet.

As if riveted to the floor, Fin watched him remove his wide-brimmed hat and shrug out of his western jacket, then toss them on the back of an armchair. Years of listening to her mother recite the rules of proper etiquette went right out the window when she turned and entered the kitchen.

The proper thing would have been to step forward, take his hat and coat and hang them in the closet. But when Travis had unsnapped the cuffs of his chambray shirt and started rolling up the long sleeves over his tanned, sinewy forearms, she'd quickly decided there was a lot to be said for the old adage about retreat being the better part of valor.

Just the memory of those arms holding her so tenderly as they'd succumbed to passion that night in his barn last month was enough to cause her pulse to race and her breathing to come out in short, raspy little puffs. Everything about that night had been pure magic and she'd spent the past month doing her best to forget that it ever happened.

"You've got to get hold of yourself," she muttered when she noticed her hand trembling as she spooned coffee into the basket.

"Did you say something?" he called from the living room.

"No, just talking to myself."

Closing her eyes, she shook her head in an effort

to dislodge the disturbing memory. What on earth had gotten into her?

She was editor-in-chief of one of the top fashion magazines in the world, a shark in the corporate boardroom and had the ability to send the most fearless intern running for cover with nothing more than a raised eyebrow. But in Travis's presence, she seemed to be continually reminded of the fact that she was first and foremost a woman who had ignored her feminine wants and needs in favor of a rewarding career in the publishing industry.

Only, in the past couple of months she'd begun to realize that her career wasn't nearly as satisfying as she'd once thought it to be. Since learning Jessica Clayton was her long-lost daughter and meeting Travis, Fin had been reminded of what she'd given up in order to devote herself to making *Charisma* the premier magazine of the fashion world.

When she'd been a young girl, she'd wanted nothing more than to be a wife and mother, to have a family of her own. But that dream had been shattered when Patrick had forced her to give her baby girl away and had forbade her to ever see Jessie's father again. She'd never forgiven Patrick for denying her desperate pleas to keep her child, nor had she ever gotten over the loss. After she'd returned from the convent her parents had sent her to in Canada to hide her and her "shameful" condition from social and business acquaintances, she'd thrown herself into her schooling, then later into her career in an attempt to assuage the pain.

But it hadn't worked. She sighed heavily. All that she'd accomplished was finding that as she approached middle age, she was alone, childless and had become a hopeless workaholic.

"Are you all right?"

The sound of Travis's voice caused her to jump. Spinning around, she found him leaning one broad shoulder against the doorframe, much like he'd done this afternoon in her office. "Of course, why wouldn't I be?"

He pushed away from the doorframe and took a step toward her. "You were standing there staring off into space like your mind was a million miles away."

Shaking her head, she turned to slide the filled basket into the coffeemaker, then flipped the switch. "I was just thinking about the latest accounting figures for *Charisma*," she lied. "If my staff and I work hard enough, we should still be able to pull ahead of my brother Shane and his magazine, *The Buzz*."

"I don't think so."

"You don't think we'll be able to win?" she asked, frowning.

He shrugged. "I can't say if you will or not. I was

talking about what you were thinking. Whatever it was, you looked like your best roping horse had just pulled up lame, not like you were worried about winning a contest."

Shaking her head, she hoped her laughter didn't sound as hollow to him as it did to her. "I've never even ridden a horse, let alone owned one. And as for roping, I'm afraid I'd be a hopeless failure."

"You've never ridden a horse?" he asked, clearly shocked.

Grateful that she'd successfully diverted the conversation, she shook her head. "Not unless the rocking horse I had as a child counts."

His promising grin sent a wave of heat zinging throughout her body. "Looks like the next time you visit the Silver Moon, I'll have to teach you how to do more than just drive."

She swallowed hard as she tried not to think of the many other things he could teach her. And not one of them involved any type of horsepower— mechanical or otherwise.

Before she could think of something to say that wouldn't give her inner thoughts away, there was a knock on her apartment door. "I think our dinner has arrived," she said, thankful for Mr. Chang's habit of always being punctual.

"Why don't you set the table while I take care of the delivery guy?" Travis asked, starting toward the door.

As he walked across the living room, he wondered what in the name of hell he'd been thinking when he'd taken Fin up on her offer to eat at her place. They couldn't be within twenty feet of each other for more than a couple of minutes without the sexual tension around them becoming so thick it could be cut with a knife. And just the thought of how responsive she'd been to his touch that night in his barn was enough to make his body as hard as a chunk of granite.

But no matter how strong the attraction was between them or how great the sex, nothing could ever come of it. Not only was she Jessie's biological mother, Fin Elliott was a sophisticated career woman. She was city from the top of her pretty red head all the way to her perfectly polished toenails. Her lifestyle was glitz and glamour and that was a far cry from the simple life he led in the wide open spaces on the Silver Moon Ranch. While she attended formal galas and went to trendy nightclubs, he was more apt to be going to a stock auction or stopping in at the local honky-tonk for a cold beer.

As he paid the delivery boy, Travis took a deep

breath. The best thing he could do for his peace of mind would be to remove himself from the temptation that Fin Elliott posed to his suddenly overactive libido. He'd take the food into the dining room, make his excuses and head back to his hotel for room service and a shower cold enough to make him spit ice cubes.

But a few minutes later, when he set the bag on the chrome-and-glass table, Fin's warm smile had him settling onto a chair across from her. As he watched her pull white cartons with red Chinese symbols from the sack, he counted at least six, plus a couple of foam containers and some small waxed paper bags.

"How much did you order?" he asked, skeptically eyeing the amount of food in front of them.

She stopped fussing over the lids on the containers of what looked to be some kind of soup to give him a sheepish grin. "For some reason, everything sounded so good." She caught her perfect lower lip between her teeth. "But I think I might have gotten a little carried away."

"It looks like you're getting ready to feed an army." Laughing, he reached for one of the boxes. "Lucky for you, I've always had a pretty healthy appetite."

"I normally try to watch what I eat, but lately, I've

been absolutely ravenous," she said, spooning a heaping mound of rice onto her plate.

They ate in silence for some time, but Travis took little notice of the flavorful food. His mouth had gone as dry as a desert when he watched Fin delicately nibbling on a barbecue rib. But when her index finger disappeared between her kissable lips as she sucked away the last traces of sauce, his heart stalled and he felt as if he'd taken a sucker punch to the gut.

"That was good," he lied when, several minutes later, they settled down on the couch to drink their coffee. Truth to tell, he had no idea what he'd consumed, let alone how it had tasted. But it beat the hell out of telling her the truth—that he'd been so caught up in watching her, he'd practically forgotten his own name.

"I'm sorry you missed out on your steak dinner," she said apologetically.

"I wouldn't have enjoyed it anyway." He took a sip of the worst coffee he'd ever tasted in his entire life. Placing his cup on the coffee table in front of them, he decided that Fin might be beautiful and sexy as sin, but she couldn't make coffee worth a damn.

"You wouldn't have enjoyed your dinner because you missed getting to spend time with Jessie?"

"Not really." Shaking his head, he grinned as he

stretched his arm along the back of the couch behind her. "I'd had about all I could take of old Ornery and his hovering. That more than anything will put a man off his feed."

"He was a bit much, wasn't he?" The sound of Fin's delightful laughter sent a wave of heat streaking from the top of his head all the way to the soles of his size 13 boots.

Travis nodded as he touched the silky strands of her auburn hair with his index finger. "Old Ornery crossed the line between providing good service and being a pain in the butt."

When he moved his hand to lightly stroke the satiny skin at the nape of her neck, he felt her tremble. It was only the slightest of movements, but there was no mistaking that she was feeling the same overwhelming pull that he was.

As he watched, she closed her eyes and leaned back into his touch. "You know what Jessie was up to this evening, don't you?"

Putting his arm around Fin's slender shoulders, he pulled her closer to his side. "Our daughter is trying to set us up."

"That would be my guess." Fin's voice was softer than usual and she sounded a little breathless.

"Jess has been after me for quite a while to improve my social life." He chuckled. "Before she moved here, she even hinted that I'd been hiding out on the ranch ever since my wife died."

Fin nodded. "I've been accused of using my career to avoid becoming involved with anyone."

"Have you?" Realizing that she might be offended by his question, he shook his head. "It's really none of my business."

"I don't mind." She opened her eyes to look at him. "I haven't been using my career as an excuse. I'm just not good at relationships." She smiled. "As long as we're being honest about it, what about you? What's your excuse?"

He wasn't sure how to answer. It had taken him a few years, but he'd finally moved past the grief and accepted that he and his wife, Lauren, had been robbed of growing old together. But getting back into the dating pool seemed a little ridiculous at his age. And to be truthful about it, he hadn't really wanted to expend the energy to try.

"Some people might call it hiding out." He shrugged. "I think it's been more a case of not knowing how to be single again. I met my wife when I was nineteen years old and we were together until she passed away a few years back. If I have any dating skills left, they're pretty rusty. And besides, the rules of the game have changed quite a bit over the past thirty years."

She smiled. "Some of us were never good at the rules to begin with."

When his gaze met hers, he seriously doubted that Fin had any problems with dating protocol or with men asking her out. She most likely had them lined up from one end of the city to the other just waiting for any indication she'd be willing to grace them with her companionship.

"You're probably a lot better at it than you think, sweetheart."

Staring into her beautiful emerald eyes, Travis couldn't have stopped himself from leaning forward to press a kiss to her perfect lips if his life depended on it. But instead of the brief, friendly peck he'd intended, the feel of her lips as she kissed him back sent a wave of longing all the way to his soul and he didn't think twice about taking the kiss to the next level.

When Travis's firm masculine lips moved over hers with such tenderness that it brought tears to her eyes, Fin felt something warm and inviting blossom deep inside of her. The feeling quickly spread to fill every corner of her being. Never in all of her thirty-eight years of life could she remember a kiss being as enchanting, as compelling, as his gentle caress.

Without a thought to the consequences or the fact

that they were playing a game that could very well end in disaster, not to mention destroy her newfound relationship with Jessie, Fin didn't so much as hesitate to move closer and wrap her arms around Travis's broad shoulders. Is was totally insane, but she wanted to feel his strength surrounding her, needed to once again savor the taste of his masculine desire.

When he traced the soft fullness of her lower lip, she felt as if the blood in her veins turned to warm honey and she opened for him on a ragged sigh. Every detail of their night together in Colorado came rushing back as he tasted and explored her with tender care, and Fin felt her body tingle to life as he coaxed her to respond.

She'd never thought of herself as a sensual being, but in Travis's arms she felt more sexy, more alive than she'd ever felt in her life, and she tentatively met his demands by stroking his tongue with the tip of her own. His deep groan and the tightening of his arms around her was her reward. Feeling more feminine and powerful than she had in a very long time, she pressed herself to his wide chest. Heat flowed through her from the top of her head all the way to the tips of her toes as he stroked the tender inner recesses of her mouth. Fin could have no more stopped the insanity than she could stop her next breath.

Desire, sweet and pure, filled every cell of her being, but when he broke the kiss to nibble a path down the column of her throat, the building passion sent waves of delicious sensation coursing throughout her body. Her insides quivered and a soft moan escaped her lips as the heat flowed through her and began to gather in the pit of her stomach.

"Tell me to stop, Fin. Tell me to get the hell away from you before this goes any further," he said, his voice raspy with the same need overtaking her.

"I don't think…I can," she answered honestly.

His deep chuckle caused her to shiver with longing. "Then we may be in a heap of trouble, sweetheart, because I'm not sure I have enough strength to do the gentlemanly thing and leave on my own."

"You're right. We have a big problem, because I'm not sure I want you to be noble," she said before she could stop herself.

His chest rose and fell as he took a deep breath. "I haven't been able to forget that night back in October when you visited the ranch."

"I haven't, either."

"I don't know how it's possible, but I want you even more now than I did then."

Her breath caught and her heart skipped a beat when he slid his large hand along her ribs to the underside of her breast. "Th-this is insane."

"I couldn't agree more," he said as he cupped the soft mound through the layers of her clothing.

"I'm not good…at relationships," she reminded him when he began to trace slows circles over the tip of her sensitive breast.

"Like I told you earlier, I'm not looking for one," he said, his lips caressing the side of her neck as he spoke. "But I know what it's like to make love to you and I'd like to do it again."

"No strings attached?"

He nodded. "We've already opened that corral gate and the horse got out. I can't see the harm in having one last time together."

Resting her head against his shoulder, Fin did her best to remember all of the complications that being with this man could cause. But for the life of her, she couldn't think of a single one at the moment. And if she were perfectly honest with herself, she didn't even want to.

Before she could change her mind, she pulled from his arms, stood up and held out her hand. When he placed his callused palm on hers and rose to his feet, the look in his incredible blue eyes promised forbidden ecstasy and dark pleasure.

"One last night," she said as she led him into her bedroom and closed the door.

Three

Fin's heart raced and her knees had started to tremble, but calling a halt to what she and Travis were about to do wasn't a consideration. She felt as if she would burn to a cinder if she didn't once again feel the tenderness of his touch and experience the power of his passion.

"I know this is going to sound like I've lost my mind, but I have to know," he said, his voice low and intimate as he turned her to face him. "Are you sure about this, Fin?"

Just like everyone else, there had been several instances in her life when she'd been uncertain about her decisions. But this wasn't one of them.

"If we don't make love, I think I'll go up in flames, Travis."

"No regrets tomorrow?"

"Maybe." She caught her lower lip between her teeth to keep it from trembling a moment before she shook her head. "But not about you or our lovemaking."

She knew he was confused by her answer, but she wasn't sure how to explain what she didn't fully understand herself. How could she put into words that if she had any misgivings at all about what they were about to share, it wouldn't be about him or their night together? It was her inability to share more of herself than just her body that saddened her.

But she'd made a decision the day her father had forced her to give up her daughter. She'd vowed to concentrate on building a career that no one could take away from her. Very few men wanted to take a backseat to a woman's commitment to her work, let alone accept it and understand why she was so driven to succeed.

Of course, with Travis it was a moot point. He wasn't looking for a relationship any more than she was, nor did he have any expectations that they would ever have anything more than this one night together. Still, it seemed rather sad to think of all that she'd had to sacrifice in order to ensure her success.

Reaching up, she smoothed the lines creasing his forehead with the tip of her index finger. "Rest assured, I don't regret that night at your ranch, nor will I regret making love with you tonight."

"Then what—"

"It doesn't matter." She placed her finger to his firm lips to silence him. "Please hold me, Travis. I need you to kiss me and make love with me."

He stared at her for several long seconds as if trying to assimilate what she'd said before he took her into his arms. Slowly lowering his head to settle his mouth over hers, Travis kissed her with a thorough tenderness that brought tears to her eyes and curled her toes inside her chic black pumps.

Her pulse sped up and her stomach fluttered with anticipation when he deepened the kiss and she tasted his undeniable hunger for her. As she surrendered herself to the way he was making her feel, every nerve in her body sparked to life and a heavy warmth flowed through her veins, settling into a delicious coil deep in the pit of her belly.

As he teased her with a light stroking touch of his tongue to hers, she was vaguely aware that he'd moved his hands from her back to her waist. But when he slid his palms up over her ribs, her heart skipped several beats and her nipples tightened in anticipation of his gentle caress.

When they'd made love that night in his barn, their joining had been spontaneous and hurried—an unplanned union with the danger of being discovered. But tonight would be different. Although neither of them had intended for the evening to end with their sleeping together, tonight they had time to explore, time for the excitement of discovering what pleased each other. And they were completely alone. There was little or no possibility of anyone interrupting the coming together of two lonely souls in search of a few hours of comfort and companionship in each other's arms.

The exquisite sensations radiating from her breasts when he finally grazed the sensitive tips through her clothes sent liquid fire racing through her veins and caused her knees to wobble. The taste of his passionate kiss and the feel of his gentle touch were both thrilling and, at the same time, extremely frustrating. She wanted to feel his hands on her body without the encumbrance of satin and lace, wanted to experience the excitement of his firm lips and moist tongue savoring her sensitive skin.

"You feel so damn good," he said, raising his head. He drew in a ragged breath as he reached to turn on the bedside lamp. "But it's not enough. I'm a visual kind of guy. I want to see your beautiful body while I'm bringing you pleasure."

Captured by his intense stare, Fin felt as if he could see all the way to her soul and knew the degree of need he was creating within her. "I want to see and touch you, too, Travis."

With nothing more than a promising smile, he pulled the tail of the shirt from the waistband of his jeans, then took her hands in his and guided them to the snap closures. "Taking off each other's clothes was one of the many things we missed getting to do the first time we were together."

Her stomach fluttered with a delightful thrill at the thought of undressing him. "What else did we miss?" she asked as she unfastened the first gripper.

"We didn't get to take our time the way I would have liked," he answered, leaning forward to nibble on her earlobe.

"How long—"

"What I have in mind will take all night, sweetheart."

A shiver streaked up her spine and her fingers didn't seem to want to work as she fumbled with the next snap. "A-anything else?"

The look in his eyes seared her. "I didn't get to kiss you in ways that will make you blush from just thinking about it."

"I—I don't blush easy." Why couldn't she get her voice to work the way it should?

When he whispered what he intended to do, a jolt of pure electrified desire shot to every part of her being and she knew exactly why her vocal cords were freezing up. He was trying to send her into sensual meltdown and doing an excellent job of it.

"Is that what you want, Fin?"

Unable to get words past her suddenly dry throat, she nodded. She wanted everything this wonderful man was willing to give and had every intention of returning the favor in kind.

When she finally managed to unfasten the last snap on his shirt, she parted the chambray to gaze at his perfectly sculpted chest and stomach. A fine dusting of downy, dark blond hair covered sinew made hard from years of strenuous physical labor. She knew several male models who would kill to have Travis's muscle definition. But his perfectly padded pecs and rippling belly were results that no amount of time spent in a gym could accomplish.

"You're magnificent," she said, deciding he definitely had a point about their missing out on several enjoyable steps in the fine art of foreplay.

His low chuckle sent a wave of goose bumps shimmering over her skin. "I've been called a lot of things in my life—most of them pretty unflattering—but this is the first time anyone's ever referred to me as magnificent."

She grinned as she slipped off her shoes. "Trust me on this, darling. Your body is quite remarkable."

"I'll bet it can't hold a candle to yours," he said as he bent to pull off his boots. When he straightened he wrapped his arms around her to pull her against him. "But I'm damned sure going to find out."

His eyes held her captive as she felt his hands begin to gather the fabric of her dress. In no time at all, he pulled the clingy knit up and over her head. Then, reaching behind her, he unhooked her bra and slid the straps from her shoulders. The scrap of lace joined her dress on the floor.

When he stepped back to gaze at her, she hoped that he missed the fact that gravity had affected certain parts of her anatomy and things weren't as pert as they'd been ten years ago. Of course, they hadn't known each other then, so maybe he wouldn't notice that, although still slender and toned, she was approaching forty.

"My God, Fin, you're beautiful." From the appreciative gleam in his eyes, she had no doubt that he meant it.

Feeling more feminine and attractive than she had in a very long time, she pushed his shirt from his impossibly wide shoulders and tossed it on top of the growing pile of their clothing on the plush white carpet. Sparks of heat rushed through her at the speed of light when he pulled her back into his arms, and she had to force herself to breathe at the first contact of sensitive feminine skin meeting hair-roughened male flesh.

"You feel as good as I knew you would," he said, his breathing sounding quite labored.

"So…do…you." He wasn't the only one having trouble catching his breath.

His large hands splaying over her back felt absolutely wonderful and she marveled at how exciting his callused palms felt on her smooth skin. Closing her eyes, she reveled in the tiny tingles skipping through her at his touch. But when he leaned back to kiss the slopes of her breasts, the coil of need deep in her feminine core tightened to an empty ache and she felt as if she would melt into a puddle.

His firm lips nibbled and teased until she thought she would go mad if he didn't take the tightened tip into his mouth. But the moment his mouth closed over her, Fin's knees gave way and she had to grasp his hard biceps to keep from falling into an undignified heap at his feet.

"Easy, sweetheart." His lips grazing her sensitive

nipple as he spoke intensified the sensations racing through her body and she barely managed to suppress a moan from escaping. "We're just getting started."

"You really meant it…when you said our lovemaking would take…all night," she said, struggling to draw air into her lungs.

He raised his head, the promise in his dark blue gaze causing her heart to pound against her ribs. "I'm going to take my time and by tomorrow morning there won't be a single inch of you that I haven't kissed or made love to." His smile sent an arrow of heat straight to the most feminine part of her. "I'm not from New York, Fin. I'm a country boy with country ways. I take my time and don't get in a rush about much of anything. And especially when I'm loving a woman."

The sound of his smooth, steady baritone and the vow she detected in his navy eyes made her insides feel as if they'd turned to warm pudding. "Th-there won't be anything left of me but a pile of ashes," she said, barely recognizing the sultry female voice as her own.

His sexy grin as he guided her hands to his belt buckle increased the heat building inside of her. "Then I guess we'll go up in a blaze of glory together, sweetheart."

Slowly unbuckling the leather strap, Fin concentrated on unfastening the metal button at his waist. She delighted in the shudder that ran through his big body when her fingers brushed the bulge straining against his fly as she reached for the tab of his zipper. But instead of easing the closure open, she decided to treat him to a bit of the sweet torture he'd been putting her through.

"I think I'm going to enjoy this slow, country lovemaking," she said as she leisurely ran her finger along the top of his waistband. She allowed her knuckles to lightly brush his skin and watched his stomach muscles contract in response.

"I don't want you get the wrong idea." He drew in a deep breath. "I swear I'm not trying to hurry things along, but these jeans are getting damned uncomfortable in the stride."

"It does appear that you have a problem in that area," she teased. Taking pity on him, she eased the zipper down. "Does that feel better?"

"Oh, yeah." Brushing her fingers aside, he stepped back and made quick work of removing the denim from his muscular thighs. "You have no idea how painful a pair of jeans can be to a man in my condition."

When he straightened and reached for her, he hooked his thumbs in the elastic just below her waist. "As good as you look in this little scrap of satin, I think you'll look even better out of it," he said as he pulled her bikini panties down.

Her legs trembled and she had to brace her hands on his shoulders to steady herself as she stepped out of them. When she finally found her voice, she reached for the band at the top of his cotton briefs. "By the same token, I think you'll look fantastic out of these."

When she removed the last barrier separating them, her eyes widened and it felt as if the temperature in the room went up several degrees. That night in his barn they'd been in the shadows and there had been little time to pay attention to anything but their hurried coming together. But now she had the opportunity to study his incredible body and the perfection that was Travis Clayton.

His long legs and lean flanks were as well-defined as his upper torso, but it was the sight of his full erection that sent a shiver of anticipation and need straight to the heart of her femininity. He was an impressively built male, heavily aroused and looking at her as if she were the most desirable creature he'd ever seen.

"You may make me out to be a liar, sweetheart," he said, reaching for her.

"Why do you say that?" she asked, feeling as if

she'd go up in flames at the feel of his body touching her from shoulders to knees.

"I promised you I was going to love you all night, but now I'm not sure that's going to be an option." He shook his head. "Just the sight of you has me hotter than a two-dollar pistol in a skid row pawnshop on Saturday night."

"That makes two of us." Her body quivered at the feel of his hard arousal pressed to her lower stomach. "I feel as if I'm going to go up in flames at any moment."

"I think we'd better take this to bed, while we still have the strength to get there," he said, swinging her up into his arms.

Smiling, Fin draped her arms around his neck. "I could have walked. The bed is only a few feet away."

He gave her a quick kiss and shook his head. "I know. But that would have required me turning loose of you and I didn't want to do that."

His candidness caused her heart to skip a beat. He knew just what to say to make her feel special and cherished. But more than that, she sensed that he really meant what he said. He didn't want to let her go and she didn't want him to.

When they reached the bed, he lowered her enough to pull back the black satin comforter, then placed her gently in the middle of the queen-size mattress. She watched him retrieve something from his jeans, then slide it under the pillow a moment before he stretched out beside her.

He gathered her to him and fused their lips in a kiss that caused her head to spin. She tasted his urgent male hunger and the depth of his passion and marveled at the fact that she was the object of this amazing man's desire.

As he broke the kiss to nibble his way down to her collarbone, Fin drew in a ragged breath. But when he continued to the slope of her breast, then on to the hardened peak, her breath caught. At the first touch of his tongue to her sensitive flesh, she held his head to her and wondered if she'd ever breathe again.

Taking her nipple into his mouth, he gently sucked and teased as he slid his hand down her side, then along her outer thigh. The delicious tension deep inside of her increased to an almost unbearable ache, but when he moved his palm up the inside of her leg to her nest of feminine curls, a jolt of need stronger than she could've ever imagined raced to every fiber of her being.

But nothing could have prepared her for the level of excitement Travis created within her when he parted her soft folds and, with a feather-light touch, stroked the tiny node hidden there. Her heart pounded against her ribs and she moved restlessly against him as wave after wave of intense sensation coursed through her.

Travis was taking her to heights of passion she'd never known existed and she was certain she'd spontaneously combust if he didn't make love to her soon.

"Please, Travis…I can't…take much more."

"What do you need, Fin?"

Driven to distraction by his continued stroking and the feel of his warm, moist lips brushing the puckered tip of her breast as he spoke, she had to concentrate hard on what she needed to tell him. "I need you…to make love to me. Now!"

"But I'm just getting started, sweetheart," he said, stroking her more deeply.

"I'll never…survive."

"Are you sure?"

"Yes."

Reaching down between them, she found him and used her palm to measure his length and the strength of his need for her. When a groan rumbled up from deep in his chest and his big body shuddered against her, she was overcome by a need like nothing she'd ever known.

He caught her hands in his to stop her. "I get the idea, sweetheart."

His breathing was labored as he moved away from her to find the foil packet he'd tucked under the pillow earlier. When he'd arranged their protection, he rose over her to nudge her knees apart and settle himself between her thighs.

"Let's do this together," he said, smiling as he took her hand in his and helped her guide him.

His gaze held hers captive as together they became one and Fin knew she'd never experienced anything quite so sensual or erotic. But as he eased his hips forward and her body stretched to welcome him, she gave herself up to the delicious feeling of their joining and abandoned all other thought.

She watched his jaw tighten as he moved farther into her. "You feel so damn good, sweetheart."

"So do you," she said, wrapping her arms around his broad back and her legs around his slender hips.

When he was buried completely within her, his heated gaze held hers as he set a slow pace of rhythmic thrusts. The weight of his lower body pressed intimately to hers and the exquisite friction of their movements sent tingling sparks skipping over every nerve in her body and in no time she felt the coil in the pit of her stomach tighten to the breaking point.

Holding him to her, Fin fought to prolong the feeling of being one with this amazing man. But all too soon the tension inside of her shattered into a million shards of sensation and she moaned his name as the sweet waves of release coursed through her.

Her satisfaction must have taken him over the edge because a moment later Travis's big body stiffened, then surged into her one final time as he released his essence with a shuddering groan.

As the light of dawn began to creep into the room, Travis lay holding Fin's slight body to his side. After making love again sometime in the middle of night, she'd drifted off. But he'd lain awake, thinking about one of, if not the most, exciting encounters of his life.

When Lauren had been alive, their coming together had been that of two people comfortable with each other. And although their intimacy hadn't been overly passionate, it had been satisfying.

But what he shared with Fin was nothing short of explosive. Her unbridled responses to his lovemaking fueled a fire within him that he'd never imagined possible. Hell, she made him feel more like a randy teenager than a man staring long and hard at fifty.

It was a real shame that with the coming of morning their time together would end. She'd resume her life as the glamorous editor-in-chief of a fashion magazine, while he went back to being a

Colorado rancher, chasing a herd of cattle all over hell's half acre.

When Fin moaned and stirred next to him, he glanced down to find her satiny cheeks had turned ashen and her emerald eyes were clouded by a mist of tears. "What's wrong, sweetheart?"

He watched her close her eyes and swallow hard. "I think…I'm going to…be sick." She'd no sooner gotten the words past her pale lips than she was bolting from the bed and running for the adjoining bathroom.

Following her, he supported her shoulders as she sank to her knees and lost her battle with the nausea. When she finally raised her head to take a breath, he released her long enough to grab a plush terry washcloth from a rack by the shower and dampen it with cool water.

"Th-thank you," she whispered brokenly as he bathed away the beads of perspiration from her forehead and helped her into the robe that had been hanging on the back of the bathroom door.

"Feeling better now?" When she nodded, he helped her to her feet and led her back to bed. "Do you have some seltzer?"

"I think there's some club soda…in the refrigerator behind…the wet bar," she said haltingly.

Quickly pulling on his jeans, Travis hurried into the other room. When he returned to the bedroom, he found her once again paying homage to the porcelain god.

"Do you think it was something you ate that didn't set well?" he asked as he knelt beside her and helped her take a few sips of club soda.

She shrugged her slender shoulders. "I've been queasy a lot lately, but this is the first time I've been sick."

Her words slammed into him like a physical blow and he had to force himself to breathe. "How long has this been going on?"

"I don't know," she said weakly. "Maybe a couple of weeks. I've been meaning to make an appointment with my doctor, but haven't gotten around to it."

His heart raced and a knot began to form in the pit of his stomach. "Have you had a period since you returned from your trip to the Silver Moon?"

As he watched her worry her lower lip between her teeth, he knew the answer even before she managed to get the single word out. "No."

The timing was right and the fact that they'd failed to use any kind of protection that night in his barn left him with only one conclusion. Taking one deep breath, then another, Travis felt light-headed and just a little queasy himself.

"Fin, I think there's a damned good possibility that you're pregnant with my baby."

Four

When the gravity of the situation finally began to settle in, Travis's words were as effective as a dose of smelling salts to Fin's cloudy brain. For the past week, she had purposely denied the telltale symptoms of pregnancy, but it was past time that she faced the facts.

She'd rationalized the occasional light-headedness and morning nausea as the result of stress from the competition and working grueling hours to win. But apparently that wasn't the case. It appeared that history was repeating itself and she was pregnant again after only one incidence of unprotected sex.

"This can't be happening," she moaned, burying her head in her hands. "Not again."

"It's going to be all right, Fin. Until you take a pregnancy test, we won't know for sure," Travis said, his voice gentle as he lifted her to his wide chest and carried her back into the bedroom. When he placed her on the bed, he sat down beside her and took her hands in his. "If you'll tell me where the nearest drug store is located, I'll run out and buy one of those home tests. Once we get the results, we'll know what we're facing and figure out how to handle it."

She raised her gaze to meet his. "We?"

He nodded without so much as a moment's hesitation. "If you are carrying my baby, you're not going to face the music alone. I'll be there with you every step of the way and whatever decisions have to be made, we'll make them together."

His vow to lend his moral support was very much appreciated, but until the stick turned blue, she had every intention of holding out hope that she wasn't pregnant. "Let's get that test kit and find out for certain one way or the other."

Giving Travis her key to let himself back in and directions to a pharmacy close by, she waited until he left before she allowed her tears to fall.

What on earth had she gotten herself into this time? And could the timing have been any worse?

She was in a fierce competition with her family, and especially her twin, Shane, to be named CEO of Elliott Publication Holdings when Patrick retired in a couple of months. Even if *Charisma*'s growth pushed it over the top and she became the clear winner of the contest, she seriously doubted that her self-righteous father would turn over the reins of his magazine empire to the daughter who made a habit of disgracing him with grandchildren born out of wedlock. And although times were different than they'd been twenty-three years ago and it was perfectly acceptable for a single woman to bear and raise her children alone, Patrick was from a different generation. There was no way he'd hand over his precious company to a woman he considered unable to manage her own life.

Her breath caught on a sob and she squeezed her eyes shut as she thought of all she stood to lose. "J-Jessie," she said aloud.

What would this do to her fledgling relationship with her daughter? They'd just found each other. How would Jessica react to the news that her biological mother and adoptive father had been unable to control themselves and now she was going to have a baby brother or sister?

Leaning back against her pillows, Fin tried not to think of the fallout an unplanned pregnancy would cause if what she and Travis suspected was true. The implications were endless and just thinking about them made her temples throb and a heavy feeling of dread fill her chest.

When she heard Travis unlock her apartment door, she sat up and wiped the moisture from her cheeks. She was no longer that frightened fifteen-year-old girl who'd had no recourse but to go along with whatever decision her parents made for her. She was a woman now and no matter what results the test showed, she would handle the situation with dignity, grace and a strength of will that she hadn't possessed twenty-three years ago.

"Is it showing anything yet?" Travis asked as he paced outside of Fin's bathroom door.

The pharmacist he'd talked to had assured him that the pregnancy test kit he purchased was the easiest, most accurate over-the-counter indicator on the market. If the digital display spelled out "pregnant," then he and Fin were going to have a baby together.

His heart thudded in his chest like an out of control jackhammer every time he thought of Fin being pregnant. He never in his wildest imaginings would have thought that at the ripe old age of forty-nine, he'd be anxiously awaiting test results to see if he'd gotten a woman "in trouble."

When he heard the bathroom door open, he stopped pacing. The look on her beautiful face answered his question even before he got the words out. "You're pregnant, aren't you?"

He watched her take several deep breaths as if she needed fortification, then nodding, she walked over to sit on the side of the bed. "It was such a strong positive that it didn't even take the entire amount of time the directions said it would for the results to show up."

Before his knees gave way, he sank down on the mattress beside her, then, putting his arms around her shoulders, he tried to think of something to say. Hell, what could he say? He felt as if he'd just been hit right square between the eyes with a two-by-four.

"I don't know how you feel about all this, but I'm going to keep my baby," she said suddenly. Emphatically.

He shook his head. "I never doubted for a minute that you wouldn't."

She straightened her shoulders and turned to face him. The only indication of her turmoil was the slight trembling of her perfect lips. "Patrick forced me to give up Jessica, but this time I won't let anyone take my child."

Travis could understand why she felt the way she did, given that her parents had made her put

Jessie up for adoption. But the baby was his, too, and he fully intended to be part of his child's life.

Only now wasn't the time to start discussing shared custody. Fin was about as fragile as he'd ever seen a woman and she needed his support. And he'd damned well give her the encouragement she needed or die trying.

"I give you my word that as long as I have breath in my body no one will separate you and the baby," he said gently.

Tears welled up in her pretty emerald eyes. "There's no way I could bear to go through that again, Travis."

"I know, sweetheart, and I promise you won't have to." He pulled her into his arms and held her close. "I'll be right beside you every step of the way and I'll walk through hellfire and back before I let anyone or anything harm you or our baby."

They sat in silence for some time before she pulled from his arms. "If you don't mind, I think I'd like to be alone for a little while."

He could understand her need for a little solitude. A lot had happened in the past hour or so and they both needed time to sort out their feelings.

"Are you going into the office today?" he asked as he rose from the side of the bed.

She shook her head. "My absence is going to

raise a few eyebrows and generate more than a little speculation, but I'll call Cade and have him take over for me today. Aside from the fact that I wouldn't be able to concentrate, I'd like to see my gynecologist as soon as possible. Hopefully, she'll be able to work me into her schedule sometime today."

As she walked him to the door, he shrugged into his coat and picked up his wide-brimmed hat. "Will you be all right on your own or do you want me to go with you to see the doctor?"

"You really meant what you said about being there for me." Her amazed expression and the sound of her voice left little doubt that he'd surprised her.

He caught her gaze with his as he touched her soft cheek with his index finger. "I never say anything that I don't mean, Fin." Giving her a quick kiss, he opened the door. "I'll be back this evening to check on you and see that you're all right."

Stepping out into the hall, he put his hat on and closed the door behind him. The last thing he wanted to do was walk away from her. But they both had a lot to think about and things they needed to do. Fin was going to try to get an appointment with her doctor and he had to call his housekeeper, Spud, to see how the ranch was faring in his absence. Then, after a quick lunch with Jessie, he had to get fitted for that damned monkey suit she was going to make him wear when he walked her down the aisle.

While he stood on the sidewalk waiting for a passing taxi, he couldn't stop thinking about the baby Fin was carrying. He shook his head in total disbelief. Most of his friends back home were becoming grandpas and here he was starting a second family.

When he and Lauren had discovered that she was unable to have children, they'd accepted the fact they would never have a child of their own and started the adoption process. And although Jessie wasn't his biological daughter, she was, and always would be, his little girl. From the moment he'd laid eyes on her bundled up like a little doll in her light pink baby blanket, she'd stolen his heart. He loved her more than life itself and that would never change.

But the baby growing inside of Fin would be his own flesh and blood—a child he never in a million years expected to have. That was going to take some getting used to, especially after all this time. It was also going to take awhile to wrap his mind around the fact that his adopted daughter and his biological child had the same mother.

And if he was struggling to come to grips with it

all, he couldn't even imagine how hard it was for Fin. Within the past couple of months, she'd found her first child and become pregnant by that child's adoptive father with her second child.

Sliding into the backseat of a taxi, he gave the driver the name of his hotel. As an afterthought, he asked, "Would you happen to know where I could order some flowers?"

"My cousin Vinnie's a florist," the man said. "His shop is a block down from your hotel. Tell him that Joe sent you. He'll give you a deal."

"Thanks, I'll do that."

Travis wasn't certain what the protocol was, or even if there was one, for waking up to find that he'd impregnated the woman he'd just spent the most incredible night of his life making love to, but he figured a nice bouquet of flowers surely wouldn't be considered offensive. He not only wanted to show Fin that he meant what he'd said about being supportive, he also wanted her to know how honored he felt that she was giving him a second go-round at fatherhood.

"What the hell's going on, Fin?" Her twin brother, Shane, barged into her apartment as soon as Fin answered the door.

"Good evening to you too, Shane," Fin said dryly.

She wasn't surprised that he stopped by on his way home from work. His apartment was only a few floors up from hers.

When he turned to face her, his expression was filled with concern. "Are you feeling all right?"

"I'm fine."

He frowned. "Then why didn't you come into the office today? I can't remember the last time you took an entire day off and neither can anyone else. Cade and Jessie have no idea what's going on and you have poor Chloe worried sick. She said you were having some problems with dizziness and she's convinced that you've worked yourself into physical exhaustion."

Fin had known that her absence would create a stir, but that couldn't be helped. "Would you like to sit down while you're taking me to task or would you prefer to stand?"

Her question seemed to erase much of the irritation from his handsome face. "Look, I'm sorry if I came across a little strong, but you'll have to admit that missing a day at *Charisma* is completely out of character for you. Especially when we're neck and neck in the competition for CEO."

Fin could understand her twin's confusion. She'd made it clear from the moment Patrick made his announcement about the contest that she had every intention of winning. But several things had changed in the past couple of months and she was having to realign her priorities.

"I appreciate everyone's concern and I truly didn't mean to cause you or anyone else any undue worry, but I had some personal business to attend to."

He cocked one dark eyebrow. "Would you care to elaborate?"

"No."

He looked taken aback. "But—"

"As I told you, it's personal."

She could tell he was more than a little mystified by her lack of details. But as close as she and Shane had always been and as much as they'd always shared, she wasn't about to discuss her pregnancy with him or anyone else. At least, not until she and Travis had the opportunity to talk things over and decide how to spring the news on everyone.

To soften her refusal to explain further, she smiled. "I'm sure there are things about yourself that you keep private, aren't there?"

A slow smile began to spread across his handsome face. "A few."

"Shall we agree to leave the matter alone, then?"

He nodded. "Agreed." As she watched, her brother turned his attention to the beautiful bouquet of two dozen long-stemmed red roses arranged in a crystal vase on top of her coffee table. "Do those have anything to do with the *personal* part of your time off?" he asked, his smile turning to a knowing grin.

Reaching down, she snatched up Travis's card before Shane had the opportunity to pluck it from the plastic pick and read it. "That, dear brother, is none of your business."

The cad threw back his head and laughed. "I'll take that as confirmation that it does."

"Don't you think it's past time that you went on up to your apartment and left me alone?"

"Expecting the sender of those flowers to show up soon, sis?" he teased. Before she could get the words out, he answered his own question. "I know, it's none of my business."

"Give the man a prize," she said, ushering him toward the door.

"All right, I'm going." Opening the door, he stepped out into the hall and turned back to face her. "Then you'll be at the office tomorrow?"

She nodded. "Of course. Where else would I be?"

His grin turn mischievous. "In the arms of whoever sent those flowers?"

"Mind your own business, Shane. And while you're at it, have a nice evening," she said, closing the door behind him.

She'd only made it halfway across the living room before a short knock had her turning back. "What part of 'it's none of your concern' don't you understand?" she asked as she jerked the door open.

"I take it that I'm not who you were expecting to see."

Fin's heart skipped a beat at the sight of Travis. He and Shane couldn't have missed each other by more than a matter of seconds.

"I'm sorry, Travis," she apologized, standing back for him to enter her apartment. "Shane felt it was his duty to give me the third degree about missing work."

He nodded as he removed his hat and coat, then tossing them onto one of the armchairs, he reached out to pull her into his arms. "Yeah, when Jess and I had lunch this afternoon, she said that you'd put Cade in charge for the day and wondered if you'd said anything about not feeling well at supper last night."

It was completely insane, considering the circumstances, but his strong arms surrounding her made her feel secure and more at peace than she could ever remember. "What did you tell her?"

"The truth."

Fearing Jessie's reaction, Fin's voice trembled. "Y-you told her I'm pregnant?"

"No." Stepping back, he kept his arm around her shoulders as he led her over to sit on the couch. "Jess asked if you'd mentioned it over supper, which you didn't. I made it a point not to say anything about knowing that the sickness thing didn't show up until this morning."

Fin breathed a sigh of relief. "I know how close you and Jessie are, but would you mind me telling her about the baby?"

"To be perfectly honest, I'd really like it if you did." He gave her a sheepish grin and hugged her close. "When Jessie was a teenager, one of my biggest fears as a father was that one day she'd tell me some pimple-faced kid had gotten her in trouble."

"Didn't you trust her?" Was Travis more like Patrick than she'd thought?

"Don't get me wrong," he said, shaking his head. "I've always had all the faith in the world in my daughter. It was the teenage boys with more hormones than good sense trying to talk the prettiest girl in the county into climbing in the back of their daddy's pickup truck that gave me nightmares."

Fin couldn't help but smile. "You're a wonderful father, Travis."

He shrugged one broad shoulder. "As hard as it

is to believe, I was a teenage boy once." He chuckled. "Hell, at the age of seventeen, I think I was hard about seventy-five percent of the time. And if the truth is known, I probably caused more than a few dads some sleepless nights myself."

If he was even half as good-looking in his youth as he was now, she could imagine that he had worried several girls' fathers. "I suppose it is rather ironic that the very thing you feared for Jessie has happened to you now."

He put some space between them in order to face her. "I know this was the last thing we expected to have happen and you have every right to blame me for not protecting you that night in the barn, but I've spent the day thinking about it." He ran his hand through his thick hair. "Hell, I haven't been able to think of anything else."

"Me, either," she said, reaching up to cup his face in her palm. "But I don't want you to think that I'm assigning blame or that I regret what's happened."

"You don't?"

"Not at all." Placing her hand on her still flat stomach, she smiled. "This is a second chance for me. I missed out on so much when I was forced to put Jessie up for adoption. I never got to see her take her first step or hear her say her first word."

"Horsey."

"Excuse me?"

His grin widened. "'Horsey' was the first thing she said."

Fin laughed. "Why doesn't that surprise me? She's always talking about her horse, Oscar."

"He loves her just as much as she loves him." Laughing, Travis shook his head. "I've never seen a horse mope around like he's on his last leg for weeks at a time, then perk up like a new colt the minute she comes home for a visit."

Uncharacteristic tears filled Fin's eyes and she cursed her hormones for making her so darned emotional. "Thank you for giving her such a wonderful childhood, Travis."

When he wiped a tear from her cheek with the pad of his thumb, her skin tingled from the contact and a warmth began to fill her chest. "Thank *you* for having her," he said, his voice sounding a little gruff. "I know that putting her up for adoption was the hardest thing you've ever had to do, but raising Jess and watching her grow up was the best thing that's ever happened to me. I wouldn't have had that if not for you."

"That's why having this baby is so important to me," she said, nodding. "I'm going to get to be a part of this baby's life the way I never was with Jessie."

She could tell by the look in his sky-blue eyes that he understood, but she noticed an underlying shadow of concern there as well. Anticipating what bothered him, she rushed to alleviate his fears. "I want you to be part of his or her life, too. You're the baby's father and I would never deny you your child."

The doubt disappeared immediately and she could tell he was relieved to hear that she wasn't going to cut him out of the picture. "How are we going to handle this? With you living here in New York and me living in Colorado, it's going to take some work."

"I'm not sure," she said honestly. "But we have eight months to discuss it and make plans."

"With Jessie and Cade's wedding coming up, the next couple of weeks are going to be pretty busy." He drew her into his arms, then leaned back against the couch. "What do you say we postpone any serious discussion until after the ceremony? That will give us a little time to think about it and see what we can come up with."

"That sounds like an excellent idea. And in the meantime, I'll find a way to break the news to Jessie." Snuggling against his shoulder, she hid a yawn behind her hand. "How do you think she'll react?"

His wide chest rose and fell a moment before he tightened his arms around her. "Your guess is as good as mine, sweetheart."

Five

Fin stared at the young woman seated across from her at the dining room table and wondered how on earth she was going to broach the subject of her pregnancy. To say she was a nervous wreck was an understatement.

She and Travis had hoped she'd have the chance to talk to Jessie before he left to go back to Colorado. Unfortunately, with the approaching wedding and all the last-minute details to pull together, there hadn't been enough time.

But when she learned that Cade was flying to the west coast for a few days to wrap up a lucrative advertising deal for *Charisma* the week before the wedding, Fin seized the opportunity and asked Jessie to have dinner with her.

"Fin, our relationship means a lot to me and I want it to continue to grow," Jessie said without preamble. Fin watched her lay her fork down and catch her lower lip between her teeth as if trying to gather her courage. Then, taking a deep breath, she asked, "Have I upset or offended you in any way?"

Her daughter's question was the last thing Fin expected and she hurried to put Jessie's mind at ease. "No, honey. You haven't done anything." She covered Jessie's hand with hers. "I know we've missed out on so much over the years, but you're still my daughter. I love you. You could never do anything that would change that."

"Thank God."

The relief on Jessie's face tore at Fin's heart. She hated that she'd caused her daughter any undue worry. But she wasn't sure how long the euphoria would last once Jessie learned about Fin's pregnancy and who the father was.

"You haven't been yourself since I canceled dinner with you and Dad last week." Jessie gave her a guilty smile. "I thought you might have been angry with me for trying to set you up with Dad."

Fin's heart beat double-time. This was her opening. She just hoped her announcement didn't cause irreparable damage to Jessie's feelings for her.

"I need to talk to you about that." Fin folded her napkin and placed it on the table, then rose to her feet and motioned toward the living room. "Let's get comfortable."

Jessie suddenly looked apprehensive. "You're beginning to frighten me, Fin."

As she led the way over to the sofa, Fin shook her head. "There's absolutely no reason for you to be afraid, honey." I, on the other hand, have every reason to be scared to death, she thought, dreading what she was about to tell her daughter.

Once they were curled into opposite corners of the plush sofa, facing each other, Fin took a deep breath. "If I've been a bit distracted lately, it's because something has happened—"

"Are you all right?" Jessie interrupted anxiously.

"I'm fine, sweetie." Fin hoped her smile was reassuring, but she was so nervous, she couldn't be sure. "In fact, when I saw the doctor last week, she said I'm in perfect health."

"Then what's the problem?" Jessie asked, clearly confused.

"It's not a problem as far as I'm concerned." Fin couldn't help but smile. "It was a shock at first, but

I've had time to get used to the idea and I'm actually quite happy about it." Taking a deep breath, she met her daughter's curious gaze head-on. "I'm pregnant."

Jessie's eyes widened and she covered her mouth with her hands as she let loose with a delighted little cry. "Fin, that's wonderful." She shook her head. "I didn't even know you were involved with anyone."

"I'm not...exactly." The next part of her announcement was what Fin had dreaded most—telling Jessie who the father was. "Travis is the father."

Jessie's mouth dropped open and she stared at Fin for several long seconds. "My dad? Your baby's father is my dad? My dad, Travis? Travis Clayton?"

Fin nodded slowly. She couldn't tell if Jessie kept repeating Travis's name out of shock or revulsion.

"It was that night at the Silver Moon, wasn't it?" Jessie guessed, her expression giving nothing away. "The two of you left the party to go into the barn to check on that mare and new colt."

Nodding, Fin tried to explain. "I gave Travis a hug to show my appreciation for raising and taking such good care of you and...it just happened."

"This is wonderful," Jessie said suddenly, leaping forward to throw her arms around Fin. "I suspected that something was going on between the two of you." Leaning back, she beamed. "I could see the attraction from the moment you met."

"You're not upset?" Fin asked cautiously as she hugged her back.

Jessie shook her head and sat back to give her an encouraging smile. "I'll admit that it's a huge shock, but I'm thrilled for both of you. I know how much you missed getting to see me grow up and Dad is the best father, ever. This baby is extremely lucky to have the two of you for parents."

Relief washed through Fin at Jessie's emphatic tone, leaving her feeling weak and emotional. "I'm so glad to hear you aren't upset."

"Why would I be upset? I'm ecstatic that I'm finally going to have a sibling," Jessie said, grinning from ear to ear. "And I'll bet Dad is excited beyond words." She stopped suddenly. "You have told him, haven't you?"

Fin nodded. "I discovered that I'm pregnant last week, while he was in town visiting and getting the last fitting for his tux." She purposely omitted they were together when she'd taken the pregnancy test and the fact that they'd spent the night before making love.

"I wonder why Dad hasn't said anything."

"I asked him to let me tell you about the baby because if our predicament upset you, I wanted the brunt of your anger directed at me," Fin explained. "I thought if I took the majority of the blame it would keep from damaging your relationship with your father."

Jessie reached out and took Fin's hands in hers. "That is so sweet of you. But I'm in no way upset by this." She grinned. "Far from it."

Fin felt as if a huge weight had been lifted from her shoulders. "You don't know how many times I've wanted to talk to you about this, but there was never a good time."

"Everything has been so busy with the wedding and all, I'm surprised we were able to find time to have dinner this evening," Jessie agreed, nodding. "Have you told anyone else?"

"No. We felt that you should be the first to know."

"I know I'm just full of questions," Jessie said, her expression turning serious, "but have you made any decisions about how you're going to raise the baby? Are you going to try to share the responsibility?"

"It's only fair that we do." Fin sighed. "But I have no idea how we're going to work this out."

"You have *Charisma* and I can't see Dad leaving the Silver Moon to move to New York," Jessie said, shaking her head.

"We're going to review our options while he's

here for the wedding and hopefully come up with a workable plan." Smiling, Fin reached out to hug her beautiful, understanding daughter. "Keep your fingers crossed that we find a solution and that when we make the announcement about my impending motherhood the rest of the family is as enthusiastic as we are."

Tears filled Fin's eyes as she watched Travis, looking incredibly handsome in his black tux, escort their beautiful daughter down the sweeping stair-case at The Tides. Jessie was utterly stunning in her pure white satin-and-lace wedding gown and if the captivated look on Cade's face was any indication, the groom thought so, too.

Glancing over at her mother and Patrick, Fin was thankful they'd welcomed their long-lost grand-daughter back into the Elliott clan and insisted the wedding be held at their estate in the Hamptons. All things considered, it was the very least they could do for Jessie.

When Travis walked his daughter down the aisle between the rows of chairs assembled in the large living room, Fin's heart went out to him as he kissed Jessie's cheek, then stepped back for Cade to take his place beside her. It had to be one of the most dif-ficult things Travis had ever had to do—placing the care and happiness of his beloved child in the hands of someone else.

"That was tough," he whispered, his voice gruff as he sat in the seat beside her to watch Jessie and Cade exchange vows.

Unable to get words past the lump clogging her throat, Fin reached over to give his hand a gentle squeeze. She wasn't at all surprised when he held onto it as the ceremony proceeded.

By the time Jessie and Cade had been pronounced husband and wife and everyone started making their way to the heated tent that had been adjoined to the family room to accommodate the reception, Fin needed a few moments alone to collect herself. "If you'll excuse me, Travis, I think I need to freshen my makeup."

"I could use a couple of minutes myself," he said, his need for solitude reflected in his tight expression and the gruff tone of his voice. "If you don't mind, I think I'll step outside to catch my breath."

"I'll see you a bit later," she said, kissing his lean cheek.

As she stood watching Travis walk to the front door, she couldn't help but wonder what it felt like to have a father who loved his child as much as Travis loved Jessie. She'd never had that, never known what it was to have a father who loved unconditionally. Placing her hand over her stomach, she knew her baby was extremely lucky to have Travis for his or her father.

"Fin, are you feeling well? I noticed you look a bit pale."

At the sound of the soft Irish lilt beside her, Fin glanced over at Maeve Elliott. "Mom, could we speak in private?" she asked, deciding there was no time like the present to tell her mother about the baby.

A look of alarm widened Maeve's soft green eyes and Fin knew her mother anticipated bad news. "Of course, dear." Leading the way into the library, she closed the door behind them. "What is it, Finola? What's wrong?" The use of Fin's given name was an indication of the level of Maeve's concern.

"There's nothing wrong," Fin said, placing her hand on her mother's arm to reassure her. "Actually, everything is the way it should be for the first time in twenty-three years."

The worry lines creasing her mother's kind face softened into a smile and she gathered Fin into her arms. "'Tis the way I feel, too, Finny."

Fin held onto her mother for several moments before she led her over to the tall leather armchairs facing the fireplace. "Please sit down, Mom. I have something I need to tell you." When they were both seated in the comfortable chairs, Fin met her mother's questioning gaze. "I'm pregnant. I'm going to have a baby with Jessie's adoptive father, Travis."

Maeve stared at her a moment before covering her eyes and breaking into soft sobs.

A feeling of déjà vu swept over Fin. Her mother's reaction was much the same as it had been the night Fin had told her she was pregnant with Jessie. The only difference between then and now was that Patrick wasn't present for this announcement.

"I had hoped you would be happy for me this time," Fin said, sighing heavily. "But it appears that I've once again disappointed you."

"Oh, no, Finny." Her mother reached out to take Fin's hands in hers. "My tears are those of joy. You never got to hold Jessie, to watch her grow into a beautiful young woman. 'Tis past time that you got to hold and raise a wee babe of your own."

"I should have been allowed to raise Jessie." Try as she might, Fin couldn't keep her bitter tears in check. "Why, Mom? Why didn't you stop Patrick from forcing me to give my baby away? You of all people should have known what it felt like to lose your child. To have her taken away without being able to…stop it from happening." Struggling to control her voice, she shook her head. "Didn't you feel as if your heart had been ripped from your chest when Anna died?"

The emotional pain that clouded Maeve's eyes tore at Fin's heart. She hadn't meant to mention her sister. It had to have been devastating for her mother to lose a seven-year-old child to cancer, but what Fin said was true. Maeve should have known what it would be like for Fin to have her baby taken from her with no say in the matter.

"Oh, Finny, 'tis sorry I am that you had to go through that," Maeve said, her Irish accent becoming more pronounced, as it always did when she was upset or overly emotional. Wiping her tears with a linen handkerchief, she shook her head. "'Twas a sad day for this family and one I have regretted all these years since."

"Then why did you let Patrick do that to me? Couldn't you have stopped him?"

Her mother shook her head. "I did try. But your da wouldn't listen and when it became a threat to our marriage, I backed down."

"You and Patrick had problems because of my situation?" It was the first Fin had heard of it if they had.

Maeve nodded. "Your da is a stubborn man. He put his pride ahead of what was right for you and this family."

"I never knew." Fin had always thought her mother supported every decision Patrick made. "The two of you always presented a united front and I thought you let him force me to give up my child without lifting a finger to help me."

"'Twasn't for you to know," Maeve said, smiling sadly. "What happens between a husband and wife behind closed doors is no one's affair but their own."

"I'm so sorry, Mom." Letting go of the last traces of her misguided anger at her mother, Fin knelt down and put her arms around Maeve's thin shoulders. "I know how much you've always loved Patrick. It must have torn you apart to be caught in the middle of all that."

"'Tis done and past." Her mother soothingly stroked Fin's hair. "Since we are all gathered for Jessie's wedding, I think you should tell the family about the wee one you carry," she said softly as they continued to embrace.

Leaning back, Fin shook her head. "I don't think it's the right time. This is Jessie's day and I don't want to cause a scene or detract from her happiness in any way."

"Does she know?"

Fin nodded. "I didn't want her to hear it from someone else."

"Was she happy for you and her da?"

"She's thrilled."

"'Tis rare when we all gather at the same time." Smiling, Maeve rose to her feet, then tugged on Fin's hand for her to stand. "We should celebrate a new babe on the way, as well as a wedding."

Fin tried to swallow her apprehension. "I don't want Patrick ruining this day for Jessie because of me."

Maeve shook her head. "You needn't worry, Finny. Your da is different now."

"Since when?"

"Give him a chance," Maeve said, her smile encouraging.

As they walked out of the library and down the hall, Fin found Travis standing by the staircase. She needed to warn him about her mother's request, as well as find Jessie and Cade and see if they had any objections to her announcing her pregnancy.

"We'll join the reception in a moment, Mom," Fin said, waiting until Maeve disappeared down the hall before she turned to Travis. "Since everyone is here, my mother thinks we should tell the family about the baby," she said, careful to keep her voice low. "Are you okay with that?"

He nodded. "I'm fine with it. The question is, how do you feel about it?"

"I'm not sure," she said truthfully. "I couldn't be

more excited and I want to tell everyone how happy I am that I've been given a second chance at motherhood. But at the same time, I'm apprehensive about Patrick's reaction. I don't want him putting a damper on Jessie and Cade's big day."

Travis shook his head. "He won't."

"You don't know Patrick Elliott the way I do." She sighed. "And thank your lucky stars you don't."

"He's all about appearances, isn't he?"

"That's *all* he's about," she said, unable to keep the disgust from her voice.

Nodding, Travis smiled. "Then don't you think he'll keep his mouth shut to keep from airing the family laundry in front of all these people?"

The more she thought about it, the more she realized that Travis was right. Not all of the guests were family. And Patrick would never dream of saying anything in front of outsiders that would throw the family in what he perceived to be a bad light.

"You might have a point."

Touching her elbow, he guided her toward the happy sounds coming from the direction of the reception. "Let's find Jess and Cade and clear it with them."

"I want you to promise me you'll let me know if this yahoo doesn't treat you right," Travis said as he and Jessie moved around the dance floor during the father-daughter dance. "I'll hop the first plane east and by the time I'm done with him, there won't be enough of him left to snore."

"Oh, Dad, you're such a cowboy," Jessie said, laughing and hugging him close.

He hugged her back. "I just want you to be happy, angel."

"The only thing that would make me happier would be if Mom was here," she said softly.

Time had eased his loss, but he hated that Lauren couldn't have been here to see their little girl on her special day. "Your mom would have been right in the middle of all this fuss and loving every minute of it."

A tear slipped down Jessie's cheek. "I know."

They were silent for a moment before he asked, "Are you and Cade sure you're all right with Fin letting the family know about the baby here at the reception?"

She nodded. "I think this is the perfect time. In fact, if you don't mind, I'd like to have the honor of telling everyone. Do you think Fin would mind?"

"To tell the truth, I think she'd be relieved that someone else let the cat out the bag." Travis glanced over at the Elliott patriarch. "She's dreading the head honcho's reaction."

"I can't imagine Fin being afraid of anything," Jessie said, frowning.

"I don't think it's a matter of her being frightened as much as it is a case of nerves," he corrected. "She just wants this day to be perfect for you and Cade." He chuckled. "I have a feeling if old moneybags over there gets his drawers in a wad, she'll take into him like a she-bear protecting her cub."

Jessie smiled fondly. "That's so sweet of her." She paused for a moment. "I don't think Granddad will say a single word after I make the announcement. You just stick close to Fin. I'm sure she could use all the moral support she can get."

Travis had no idea what Jess had planned, but she had a good head on her shoulders. He trusted her judgment and if she said she could spring the news and keep Elliott from raising a ruckus, he had no doubt she could do it.

"All right, angel. This is your day. Do what you think is best."

When the dance ended, Travis kissed her cheek and, stepping back for Cade to take his place, walked over to sit at the table with Fin and Shane. "Jessie's going to take care of telling everyone the big secret," he said close to Fin's ear. "Any objections?"

She shook her head and her silky auburn hair

brushing her creamy shoulders fascinated the hell out of him. "I don't mind, but when is she going to do it?"

"Your guess is as good as mine." He covered her hand where it rested on the white linen tablecloth. "But if I know Jess, it won't be long."

He'd no sooner gotten the words out than Jessie and Cade walked over to one of the band's microphones. "If I could have your attention, my wife has an announcement to make," Cade said, giving Jessie a look that left Travis with no worries about how much he adored her.

When all eyes turned her way and the room fell silent, Jessie gazed lovingly at the man standing beside her. "This is one of the happiest days of our lives and Cade and I would like to thank you all for helping us celebrate our marriage." Turning her attention toward the table where Travis sat with Fin, she smiled. "I would also like to announce that we have another reason to celebrate. My dream of being a big sister is finally going to come true. Fin and my dad have just learned they're going to give me a brother or sister in the summer."

The stunned silence that followed was suddenly interrupted by a round of applause and Travis found himself and Fin besieged by a herd of well-wishing Elliotts. As Fin's brothers, their wives and what seemed like an endless line of nieces and nephews congratulated them, he couldn't help but notice that Fin's gaze kept returning to the tall, silent, white-haired gentleman standing as stiff and straight as a marble statue on the opposite side of the room.

It appeared that Patrick Elliott was none too happy about the news, even though his wife, Maeve, looked just the opposite. As Travis watched, Maeve said something to Patrick, then took the old gent by the arm and led him toward the crowd congratulating them. Putting his arm around Fin's shoulders, Travis drew her close as he met the older man's steely gaze head on, sending a clear message that Travis wasn't going to tolerate Fin being bullied or upset in any way.

When the elder Elliott approached, it was like watching the parting of the Red Sea. The family divided into two groups, and just as Travis imagined happened thousands of years ago, a hushed silence reigned. Not even the smallest child present made a sound.

"A wee babe is a grand event and we welcome another addition to the family," Maeve said, breaking the uncomfortable silence.

Stepping forward, Fin smiled and hugged her mother. "Thank you, Mom."

The crowd seemed to wait for Patrick to add his

blessings, but it never came. The man remained as stoic as ever.

Although Fin's expression never changed, Travis could have sworn he saw a shadow of pain in her pretty green eyes. But it was gone in a flash, replaced with a defiance that matched her father's.

The uneasy silence was almost deafening and just when Travis thought they'd all pass out from holding their collective breath, Maeve turned to her husband. "'Tis time you told them why you put them at odds to win the company, don't you think?"

A frown creased the man's forehead as he shook his head. "Leave it be, Maeve," Patrick said gruffly. "They'll understand soon enough." And with that, the Elliott patriarch tucked his wife's hand in his arm, turned and walked away.

"Don't let the old man get you down, sis," Shane said, hugging her.

Fin didn't look the least bit surprised by her father's reaction. "I expected nothing less from him," she said, shaking her head as she hugged her twin brother in return.

As the crowd began to recede and the band commenced playing, Travis noticed a young blond-haired woman slip up beside Shane. When she whispered something in his ear, the man let out a whoop loud enough to wake the dead, then wrapped her in a bear hug and, grinning like an old possum, swung her around in a circle.

When everyone stopped to stare at them, Travis had to choke back his laughter at the red flush creeping up from Shane's collar all the way to his forehead. The little blonde beside him was just as embarrassed and looked as if she were ready to dive under the table at any moment.

"Travis Clayton, this is Rachel Adler, Shane's executive assistant," Fin said, grinning as she made the introductions.

"It was nice to meet you, Mr. Clayton," Rachel said, her cheeks still bright red. "If you'll all excuse me, I need to be going now. I'll see you at the office on Monday, Shane."

As they watched Rachel hurry to the family room door, Fin turned to her brother. "Would you care to explain that emotional display and the huge grin on your face?"

"No."

"You want to know what I think?" Fin asked.

"No, I don't care what you think," Shane said defensively.

"Tough." As she winked at Travis, her smile caused a warmth to spread throughout his chest and he didn't think he'd ever seen her look more beautiful. "I'm going to tell you anyway, dear brother."

Shane frowned. "I'd rather you didn't."

"I don't know what Rachel told you, but I think you're to the point where you'd use any excuse to finally have her in your arms," Fin said, clearly ignoring her brother.

"You, dear sister, need to shut up and mind your own business," Shane said irritably as he turned to walk away.

"You just confirmed my suspicions, Shane," Fin called after him.

For reasons he didn't even want to begin to analyze, her delightful laughter had a strange effect on Travis's insides. "Let's dance," he said suddenly, taking her by the hand to lead her out onto the dance floor.

"I thought Jessie mentioned one time that you didn't like dancing," she said, sounding a little breathless as he pulled her to him.

"I don't." He smiled at the shiver he felt course through her when he whispered, "Your brother isn't the only man here who'll use whatever excuse he can find to have the most beautiful woman in the room in his arms."

Six

"I don't think I've ever seen a more lovely couple," Fin said, settling into the back of the EPH corporate limo for the ride back to the city. She sighed happily. "Jessie was absolutely stunning."

"She looked just like you," Travis said, reaching over to take her hand in his.

"A much younger version, maybe," she said, laughing.

His smile heated her all the way to her toes. "I don't think I had the chance to tell you how sexy you look in that slinky green dress." He lightly touched the teal silk of her Versace gown with his index finger. "You and Jessie were the two most beautiful women at the wedding."

"Well, you clean up pretty good yourself, cowboy." She placed her hand on the arm of his black tuxedo. "You look incredibly handsome in formal attire, Travis."

He grunted. "I feel like a trained monkey in a side show."

"I think you're a very handsome monkey," she said, laughing.

"Well, take a good look because I won't be wearing this thing again," he said, putting his arm around her shoulders. "I'll take it home and hang it in the closet, never to see the light of day again."

"Never say never."

"I think this is one time it's a sure bet to say never." His arm tightening around her to draw her close and his low chuckle caused every cell in her body to tingle to life. "A jackass will sprout wings and fly before you see me in this thing again."

As they left the lights of The Tides behind and the intimacy of the night closed in around them, Travis reached over and pushed the button to raise the privacy panel between them and the driver. "How are you doing?" he asked. "I know today was an emotional roller coaster for you and you have to be drained."

"I probably should be, but surprisingly I'm

feeling pretty good." Slipping off her high heels in an effort to get comfortable for the two-hour drive, she added, "Now that my pregnancy is no longer a secret, I'm more relaxed than ever."

When he gathered her close, a wave of goose bumps shimmered over her arms at the feel of his warm breath stirring the fine hairs at her temple. "I told you your dad wouldn't say anything."

"There wasn't a lot he could say after Jessie made her little speech." Touched beyond words at the enthusiasm and support her daughter had shown for her pregnancy, Fin smiled. "She's going to be a wonderful big sister."

"She'll have the poor little thing spoiled rotten."

"And you won't?"

He chuckled beneath her ear and tightened his arms around her. "I didn't say I wouldn't."

They rode along in a comfortable silence for several minutes before Travis spoke again. "Have you come to any conclusions about how we can handle your pregnancy and the distance between us?"

"With all of the last-minute details for the wedding, I haven't had time." She shook her head. "What about you? Have you come up with anything?"

"No, but we're going to have to figure out something." He touched her chin with his index finger to tilt her head back. When their gazes met, he gave her a smile that had her toes curling into the thick carpet on the limo floor. "This is all pretty new for me, but when I told you I'd be there with you every step of the way, I meant it. And I wasn't just talking about raising the baby once it gets here. I intend to be there for you through the pregnancy, as well."

Before she could respond, he lowered his head and captured her lips in a kiss so gentle it brought tears to her eyes. The soft caress of his mouth as it moved over hers had her quickly feeling as if the temperature in the car had gone up several degrees. But when he coaxed her to part for him and used his tongue to mimic a more intimate mating, a spark ignited deep in her soul and the heat flowing through her veins spread throughout her body.

Sparkles of light danced behind her closed eyes and a longing began to build in the most feminine part of her when he slipped his hand inside the plunging neckline of her evening gown and pushed the built-in cup aside to caress her breast. The work-hardened calluses on his palm chafed her sensitive nipple, sending tingling streaks of pure delight to every cell of her being. But when he traced the puckered tip with his thumb, her heart skipped several beats and her breathing became extremely difficult.

As he gently rolled the peak between his thumb and forefinger, he continued to tease her inner recesses with his tongue and her insides quivered with need like nothing she'd ever known. Heaven help her, but she couldn't have stopped a tiny moan of pleasure from escaping if her life depended on it.

"Does that feel good, sweetheart?" His smooth baritone vibrated against her lips and fed the pool of desire gathering in her lower belly.

"Mmm."

Lifting her to sit on his lap, she felt the hard ridge of his erection against her thigh, and her own body's answering need left her feeling light-headed from its intensity. The tension building inside of her was maddening and she wanted nothing more than to surrender herself once again to Travis's masterful brand of lovemaking.

His groan of frustration penetrated the sensual haze surrounding her when he tried to shift them into a more comfortable position. "It's been a long time since I made out in the backseat of a car, sweetheart." He eased her back to sit beside him on the limo's plush velour seat. "And for what I want to do to you, we'll need more room than there is in the backseat of this damned limousine."

"When are you leaving to return to Colorado?" she asked breathlessly.

"Tomorrow afternoon." He kissed his way to the hollow at the base of her throat. "Spend the night with me, Fin," he said, nibbling at her wildly fluttering pulse.

If she'd stopped to think about it, she might have thought of all the reasons they should back away from whatever was going on between them. Even though they were going to have a baby together, he lived thousands of miles away on his quiet, charming ranch in Colorado and her life was in the most exciting, glamorous city in the world.

But without a second thought, she snuggled against the most incredible, giving man she'd ever met. "Your bed or mine?"

"Why the hell can't these places have regular metal keys?" Travis muttered as he fitted the little plastic card into the lock on his hotel room door.

The ride from the Hamptons to the hotel had been the longest trip of his life. Coupled with the fact that he and Fin hadn't been able to keep their hands off of each other, he was hotter than a blast furnace in the middle of an August heat wave. And Fin wasn't much better off. Her porcelain cheeks wore the blush of unfulfilled passion and he didn't think she'd ever looked sexier or more desirable.

When the tiny light on the lock finally flashed to

green, he pushed the door open and quickly ushered her inside. The door had barely swung shut before he had the light switched on and reached to pull her back into his arms.

"You know what I've discovered about these designer dresses?" he asked as he slid the back zipper down below her waist.

"What's that?" she asked, sounding as winded as he felt.

"They're designed to drive a man out of his mind with lust."

Peeling the dress from Fin's luscious upper body, he took her into his arms as the evening gown floated down to form a green pool of silk around her trim ankles. As he pressed kisses across her collarbone, then down the creamy slope of her breast, he could have cared less that he'd just sent thousands of dollars worth of dress to lie in a tangled heap on the floor.

She shivered against him when he took her pebbled coral nipple into his mouth. Tasting her sweetness, feeling the nub tighten further, he felt his lower body harden to an almost painful state.

"You're driving me insane," she said, sagging against him.

"I'm right there with you, honey." He drew in a ragged breath. "Let's get out of the rest of these glad rags before I do something stupid and rip them off of both of us."

Fin's laughter sent a shock wave of heat coursing through him at the speed of light. "At the moment, I think you're the only one with an over abundance of clothing, Mr. Clayton."

Glancing down, he grinned at the sight of her standing before him in nothing but a little triangle of lace and silk. The dress Fin had been wearing not only had a built-in bra, it had some kind of under-skirt, as well. He wasn't sure who came up with the idea of combining women's undergarments with a dress, but he'd bet his last dime that men all over the world were singing their praises.

"I think you might have a real good point there, Ms. Elliott." Tugging his shirt from the waistband of his trousers, he could have cheerfully throttled whoever thought it would be better to use studs instead of buttons on formal wear.

"Let me help you with those," she said, stepping forward.

To his relief, within no time Fin was pushing the shirt apart to place her hands on his chest. At the first contact of her soft palms on his flesh, it felt as if a bolt of lightning shot from the top of his head to the soles of his feet.

Jerking as if he'd been zapped by a cattle prod,

he shook his head and backed away from her. "I think I'd better take care of getting undressed or else the race will be over before this old horse leaves the starting gate."

"That wouldn't be good," she said, kicking out of her high heels and reaching for the elastic band that held the tiny patch of lace material covering the apex of her thighs.

When Fin tossed her panties on top of her dress, then slid beneath the covers of the king-size bed, he swallowed hard and did his best to concentrate on getting himself out of his clothes. By the time he crawled in beside her, he was breathing as if he'd run a marathon and he was pretty sure he'd just set some kind of speed record for disrobing.

As he put his arms around her and settled his mouth over hers, her eager response sent blood surging through his veins and his arousal was so intense it made him feel light-headed. He needed her with a hunger that robbed him of breath and he wanted nothing more than to join their bodies in the age-old dance of love. But what shocked him down to the core was his deep desire to join their souls— to make her his in every way.

It should have been enough to scare the living hell out of him. But the feel of her soft body pressed to his and the taste of her sweet lips as she returned his kiss made rational thought all but impossible.

As he continued to kiss her, he felt her hands slide down his chest as if she were trying to map every individual muscle. But when her fingers touched his puckered nipple, Travis broke the kiss as he struggled for his next breath. Falling back against the pillow, he clenched his back teeth together so hard he figured it would take a crowbar to pry them apart as he tried to slow his runaway libido.

"Does that feel as good to you as it does for me when you touch me like this, darling?" Fin asked.

"Oh yeah." The blood rushing through his veins caused his ears to ring and sent a flash fire straight to his groin.

If he'd had the presence of mind, he would have stopped her before things went any further, but her hands on his body felt so damned good he didn't even consider it. Then, when her hand drifted lower to trace the narrow line of hair that arrowed down to his navel and beyond, he couldn't for the life of him force words past his suddenly dry throat.

But as her talented little fingers closed around him to measure his length and girth, then teased the softness below, he felt as if his head might just fly right off his shoulders and he had to concentrate hard on maintaining what little control he had left. A wave of need stronger than anything he could ever imagine threatened to swamp him and when he finally found the strength, he caught her hands in his to stop her tender assault.

"Honey, I don't want you thinking that I don't like what you're doing because believe me, I sure as hell do." His voice sounded like a rusty gate hinge and he had to clear his throat before he could finish. "But I'm hotter than a young bull in a pen full of heifers and I'm not going to last any longer than a June frost if we don't slow down."

Wrapping her arms around him, she smiled. "I love your quaint country sayings, even if I don't always understand them."

He laughed, releasing some of the tension that held him in its grip. "One of these days, we'll have to sit down and I'll give you a crash course in cowboy lingo. But right now I have other, more pleasurable activities in mind."

With his hormones better under control, Travis lowered his head to kiss her at the same time he parted her legs with his knee and moved over her. He'd wanted to go slow, wanted their lovemaking to last. But the two-hour ride back to the city in the limo had taken its toll. By the time they'd arrived at his hotel, he and Fin were both aroused to the point of no return and taking things slow wasn't an option.

He gazed down at the woman in his arms, the woman who was carrying his child. He didn't think he'd seen a more beautiful sight than the passion glazing her emerald eyes and the soft, welcoming smile curving her lips. "Show me where you want me, Fin."

The blush of desire painting her porcelain cheeks deepened as without a word she reached down and guided him to her.

As he eased into her and her supple body took him in, his chest swelled with an emotion he wasn't ready to identify. He felt as if he'd found the other half of himself, the part he'd been missing since the death of his wife. Trying not to think about it, or what it could mean, he set a slow pace and concentrated on bringing them both the satisfaction they needed.

The feel of her surrounding him and the motion of their bodies as they rocked in perfect unison had them racing toward completion. All too soon, he felt Fin's feminine inner muscles tighten around him a moment before she found her release.

Determined to ensure her ultimate pleasure before he found his own, he thrust into her deeply and watched her eyes widen a moment before she came apart in his arms. Gathering her to him, he let go of his rapidly slipping control to join her. His body shuddered as he gave up his essence and he was certain he felt fireworks light up the darkest corners of his soul.

His breathing harsh, Travis closed his eyes and buried his face in the cloud of her dark auburn hair. He had no idea where they would go from here or how they would work out raising the child they'd created together. But he knew as surely as he knew his own name, he was going to do everything in his power to find the right answers.

And if he had his way, he'd not only be a part of the baby's life, he'd be a big part of Fin's life as well.

The following Friday afternoon, Fin sat in her office listening to Chloe fill her in on the current projections from the accounting department and the latest EPH gossip. She was normally interested in anything that could help her push *Charisma* over the top and make her the new CEO when Patrick retired. But for the past few weeks, she'd been thinking less about her fashion magazine and more about a tall, ruggedly handsome cowboy from the wilds of Colorado.

When they'd parted ways the morning after Jessie and Cade's wedding, they still hadn't arrived at any conclusions concerning the distance separating them or how they were going to handle it during her pregnancy and after the birth. In fact, they hadn't even discussed it after he'd kissed her in the back of the limo.

Her body tingled to life from just the memory of his masterful kisses, but it was the thought of their lovemaking that quickly had her insides feeling as if they'd turned to warm pudding. Their coming together might have started out as two lonely people finding comfort and physical release in each other's arms, but somewhere along the way it had changed into something far deeper, far more meaningful.

It was completely insane, considering they had nothing whatsoever in common except for the baby she carried and their love for Jessie. But Fin hadn't been able to think of anything but Travis's request that she come out to Colorado for a visit as soon as possible. And what surprised her more than anything was that she desperately wanted to go.

"Fin, have you heard a word of what I just told you?" Chloe asked. Her assistant's tone drew Fin back to the present.

"I'm sorry, I guess I was daydreaming," she apologized. She needed to get a grip on herself or she could kiss winning Patrick's contest goodbye. "What were you saying?"

Chloe's exasperated expression indicated that Fin had missed something the young woman had thought was extremely significant. "I said that you still have a good chance of beating out Shane for the CEO position." Chloe's expression changed to one of excitement. "Word around the accounting department water cooler is that *Charisma*'s numbers have closed the gap and at the rate we're going, we'll pull ahead of *The Buzz* just before the deadline."

"Really?"

A month ago, Chloe's information would have been the best news Fin could have received. It would have sent her into overdrive to make it happen and she had no doubt that it would have. But now?

She wasn't sure whether her lack of enthusiasm was due to her pregnancy and the fact that the job of CEO would keep her from devoting as much attention to her child as she knew she would want to do, or if it was the discovery that since Travis returned to his ranch, she'd been more lonely than ever before. But either way, it was clear that her priorities had changed and she was no longer as driven to be named Patrick's successor as she once had been.

"Fin, what's wrong with you?" Chloe asked, clearly confused. "I thought you'd be doing the happy dance over the news."

Smiling at her executive assistant, Fin shrugged. "I am quite pleased to hear that *Charisma* is doing so well. And I hope with all my heart that we win."

"But?"

"That's it." Fin handed a stack of ad copy to the woman and motioned toward the door. "Put these on Cade's desk with a note for him to look over them as soon as he and Jessie return from their honeymoon."

She could understand Chloe's confusion as she scooped up the stack of papers and quietly left Fin's office. But that couldn't be helped. Fin wasn't about to reveal to her executive assistant, or anyone else for that matter, that she was just the same as conceding the race for CEO to Shane.

With her decision made, she swiveled her chair to gaze out at the western side of the Manhattan skyline. She really would like to win the competition, but not because she coveted Patrick's title. If *Charisma* did pull ahead of *The Buzz*, she had every intention of declining the position. But winning would certainly prove to Patrick that she wasn't quite the disappointing failure he'd always thought her to be.

Quite content with herself for the first time in years, she relaxed and thought about her lack of plans for the weekend. Her OB/GYN had advised that getting the proper amount of rest was essential to the health and well-being of both her and the baby. And for the past week, she had cut back on the hours she spent at the office. But the thought of rattling around in her huge apartment by herself for the entire weekend was extremely unappealing.

Nibbling on her lower lip, she wondered how Travis intended to spend the time. He had told her that he hoped she planned to visit the Silver Moon at her earliest convenience.

She turned her chair to face the desk, then typed a quick search into her computer. When the information she wanted appeared on the screen, she reached for the phone and dialed the number for the airlines.

When the booking agent answered, Fin's heart skipped a beat and she couldn't believe the level of excitement coursing through her as she made her request. "I need to reserve a first-class seat on the first available flight from New York to Denver, Colorado, please."

Seven

Parking his truck in short-term parking at the Denver airport, Travis impatiently checked his watch as he started walking toward the terminal. He'd been tied up in a traffic jam on the interstate while the authorities cleared away a fender bender and the longer he'd had to sit there, the more he'd realized how much he'd missed Fin since leaving New York.

It didn't matter that it had only been a few days since he'd said goodbye to her at his hotel the morning after Jessie's wedding or that they barely knew each other. It felt as if it had been an eternity since he'd seen her. And when she'd called this morning to see if he had plans for the weekend, he hadn't been able to tell her fast enough that he didn't.

He refused to think about why he was so anxious to be with her again or why he'd been as irritable as a grizzly with a sore paw since his return. All that mattered was the three days they'd have together on his remote ranch. Alone.

As soon as his housekeeper, Spud Jenkins, heard that Fin was on her way, he'd suddenly remembered that he had plans to visit his brother's family down in Santa Fe. Travis knew the old geezer had made up the excuse. Spud and his brother had been on the outs for well over twenty years. But Travis hadn't bothered to point that out to the old cowboy.

The truth was, he needed time alone with Fin to figure out what was going on between them. And he wasn't just thinking about how they were going to manage his role in her pregnancy and, later on, the raising of their child.

When he entered the baggage claim area, he spotted Fin immediately as she waited for her luggage to tumble out of a chute and onto the revolving carousel. Damn, but she looked good in a pair of jeans and that oversized tan sweater.

It was the first time he'd seen her in anything but dress clothes or formal wear and he wasn't the least bit surprised that he found her attractive in more casual attire. Hell, it didn't matter what she wore, she knocked his socks off every time he saw her.

Dodging a couple of teenagers with battered backpacks and an older woman pulling a suitcase big enough to hide a body in, he walked over to wrap his arms around Fin and lift her to him. He kissed her like a soldier returning from war and when he finally set her on her feet, they were both left gasping for some much-needed air.

"I don't remember you greeting me like this the first time I came for a visit," she said, her voice sounding breathless and sexy as hell.

He felt like a damned fool, but for the life of him he couldn't stop grinning. "We didn't have a history then, sweetheart."

She laughed as she reached for a medium-sized bag that had just come down the chute. "Your definition of history is knowing each other for a month?"

Shrugging, he reached down to take hold of the luggage before she could lift it from the carousel. "If you want to get technical, what happened yesterday is history."

As they walked through the terminal, her sweet smile sent his blood pressure up a good fifty points. "I suppose you have a point."

When they reached the automatic doors at the

exit, he shook his head. "Wait here out of the cold, while I get my truck."

"You don't have to do that," she said, taking a step forward. "I don't mind walking. I'm used to walking a lot and I'm sure it's not that far."

"It's pretty cold out there and you're not used to the altitude." He dug his truck keys from the front pocket of his jeans. "It might not be good for you or the baby."

She looked at him as if he might not be the brightest bulb in the chandelier. "Travis, being pregnant isn't a disability."

"I know that." Planting a kiss on her forehead, he smiled and shook his head. "But you're in my neck of the woods now, honey. And if I want to be a gentleman and take care of you while you're here, I'll damned well do it."

Fin snuggled into the crook of Travis's arm as they sat on the leather sofa in front of a blazing fire in the big stone fireplace in his living room. She loved the cozy feel of the Silver Moon ranch house. From the rich wood and leather furniture to the colorful Native American accents, it was warm, inviting and felt exactly the way a home was supposed to feel. Something her apartment was sorely lacking.

When she returned to New York, the first thing

she intended to do was call an interior designer to have her apartment redecorated. The ultramodern, museum look wasn't in the least bit child-friendly and she wanted a comfortable, relaxed place like the Silver Moon ranch house for her baby to call home.

"I'll give you a quarter for your thoughts," he said, resting his head against hers.

"I thought that was supposed to be a penny for your thoughts," she said, feeling more relaxed and at peace than she could ever remember.

"Inflation, sweetheart." He drew her a little closer and kissed the top of her head. "I've heard that even the tooth fairy is having to pay a buck a tooth these days."

She leaned back to look up at him. "What was the going rate when Jessie was growing up?"

"Fifty cents." His smile made her tingle all the way to her bare toes. "At least it was until she learned the fine art of negotiation."

"You're kidding."

"Nope." Chuckling, he shook his head. "One time, when I went to get her tooth from beneath her pillow and leave a couple of quarters, I found a note for the tooth fairy."

Curious to hear more about what Jessie had been like as a child, Fin asked, "What did the note say?"

"Something to the effect that since it was a little

farther back in her mouth and because she used it for chewing, she thought it was worth at least seventy-five cents."

Laughing, Fin shook her head. "She didn't."

"She sure did." He grinned. "The tooth fairy laughed so hard, he damned near woke her up."

"Did she get the seventy-five cents?"

"No, that tooth netted her a cool five bucks." He shook his head. "I figured the note alone was worth that much."

"You're a wonderful father," Fin said when they stopped laughing.

He shrugged, but she could tell from the sparkle in his incredible blue eyes that her comment pleased him. "I did what I thought was best." He kissed her cheek and placed his hand over her stomach. "The same as I'll do with this baby."

Emotion filled Fin's chest and she had to swallow around the huge lump that formed in her throat. "I'm so glad you're my baby's father."

His tender smile increased the tightness in her chest. "*Our* baby. Remember, we're in this together, Fin."

She couldn't keep a lone tear from sliding down her cheek. "Thank you."

He looked taken aback. "For what?"

Reaching up to cup his lean cheek with her hand, she smiled. "For being you."

Her stomach fluttered with anticipation at the slow, promising smile curving his firm male lips. He was going to kiss her and, if the look in his intense gaze was any indication, more.

When his mouth covered hers, Fin surrendered herself to the moment and the overwhelming sense of belonging that she'd come to associate with being in Travis's strong arms. Never in her entire existence had she felt more wanted or cherished than she did when he held her, made love to her.

It didn't seem to matter that they'd only known each other a short time or that they had very little in common. She'd never felt anything as right or as real as she did when she was with him.

Her heart pounded hard against her ribs. Was she falling in love with him?

She really didn't have a lot of experience at being in love, so she wasn't certain how it was supposed to feel. She'd been positive that she loved Jessie's young father, Sebastian Deveraux. But that had been a long time ago and she suspected every fifteen-year-old girl was convinced that she loved her first boyfriend. Unfortunately, in the years since, she'd concentrated all of her energy toward building her career instead of personal relationships and she had nothing else to compare to the way she felt about Travis now.

As his lips moved over hers, coaxing her to open for him, encouraging her to respond, she abandoned all speculation and gave herself up to the delicious sensations beginning to course through her. She could analyze her feelings once she'd returned to New York.

When he slipped inside to tease her inner recesses, sparkles of light danced behind her closed eyes. But as he stroked her tongue with his it felt as if a starburst lit the darkest corners of her soul. The hunger of his kiss, the taste of his passion, sent heat surging through her veins and made every cell in her body tingle to life.

Shivers of delight slid up her spine when she felt his hand slip beneath the bottom of her sweater to caress her abdomen, then come to rest just below her breast. Restless anticipation filled her when he paused his exploration long enough to unfasten the front clasp of her bra. She needed to feel his hands caressing her, wanted his moist kisses on her sensitive skin.

The hard muscles of his arms suddenly bunched as he lifted her, then stretched them both out on the long couch. She reveled in the rapid beating of his heart and the hard ridge of his arousal against her thigh where their legs tangled, but when he created a space between them to cover her breast with his large palm, her own pulse began to race and a moist heat began to gather at the apex of her thighs.

Needing to touch him as he touched her, she unsnapped his chambray shirt to trace the steely sinew of his broad chest and abdomen. The light sprinkling of hair covering the thick pads of his pectoral muscles tickled her palms and she marveled at the exquisite differences between a woman and a man. But when she traced his flat male nipple with the tip of her finger, the tiny nub's puckered reaction was much the same as when he touched her breasts.

His groan of pleasure thrilled her and as she continued to memorize every ridge and valley, she decided Travis's body was perfect in every way. Taut and unyielding, his muscles held a latent strength that belied his gentle touch and contrasted perfectly with the softer contours of hers.

"There isn't enough room on this damned couch to kiss and taste you the way I'd like," he said, nibbling the hollow beneath her ear.

His low drawl and the promise of his words sent quivers of excitement shimmering through her. "It is rather restrictive, isn't it?"

"Damn straight." He sat up, then pulled her up

beside him. "Let's find a place with more room to move."

"That looks inviting," she said, eyeing the colorful Native American rug on the floor in front of them. She shrugged one shoulder at his questioning expression. "I've never made love in front of a fireplace."

A slow smile began to appear on his handsome face as he glanced at the rug, then back at her. "It does look fairly comfortable, doesn't it?"

Before she had the chance to agree with his observation, he was easing them onto their knees on the floor. "I'm going to love the way your body looks in the glow from the fire," he said, switching off the lamp at the end of the couch.

With nothing but the muted light from the fire, the room suddenly became incredibly intimate, and as his smoldering gaze held her captive, he slipped his hands beneath her sweater to slowly push it upward. Raising her arms to help him slip it over her head and toss it aside, she slid the straps of her bra down her arms and handed it to him. His sharp intake of breath and the darkening of his blue eyes, made her insides quiver and her breathing grow shallow.

"I've dreamed of you like this every night since that evening in your apartment." His deep baritone, rough with passion, and his appreciative look sent a honeyed warmth flowing through her veins.

Pushing his opened shirt off his broad shoulders and down his muscular arms, she smiled as she dropped the garment on top of her clothing. "And I've dreamed of you." She placed her hands on his chest. "I've wanted to touch you like this again."

He cupped her face with his hands and kissed her deeply, letting her taste a hungry need that matched her own. "I intend to touch and taste every inch of you, sweetheart. And when I'm finished, I intend to start all over again."

As he nibbled his way down her neck to her shoulder, then her collarbone, Fin's head fell back as she lost herself to the delicious sensation of having his lips on her skin. But when his hot mouth closed over her tightened nipple and he flicked the bud with his tongue, she trembled from the waves of pleasure flowing through her and the empty ache of need beginning to form deep in her lower region.

By the time he finally lifted his head, she felt as if she'd melt into a wanton puddle at any moment. "This isn't fair. I want to kiss you like this, too."

"What do you say we get the rest of these clothes off?" he asked, standing up, then helping her to her feet.

Once he'd finished stripping both of them and

they knelt facing each other on the rug in front of the fire, he took her into his arms. The feel of skin against skin, his male hardness pressed to her female softness, sent tiny currents of electrified desire to every part of her.

"You feel so damned good," he said roughly.

Delightful shivers of excitement coursed through her at the passion in his voice. "I was just thinking the same thing about you."

The sultry quality of her voice amazed her. She'd never thought of herself as a sensual creature, but with Travis it seemed all things were possible.

When he lowered them to the rug and gazed down at her, the heated need and the promise of complete fulfillment she saw in his eyes sent hot, dizzying desire flowing to the most feminine part of her. As his mouth covered hers and he slipped his tongue between her lips the pulsing ache in her lower belly increased and she gasped from the intensity of it.

But when he trailed kisses down to the valley between her breasts, then beyond, her breath caught. Surely he wasn't going to…

"T-Travis?"

Raising his head, he gave her a look that caused her heart to skip several beats. "Do you trust me, Fin?"

Incapable of speech, she could only nod. No other man had ever made love to her the way Travis was doing now and heaven help her she never wanted it to end.

As his lips blazed a trail down her abdomen, she closed her eyes and tried her best to remember to breathe as wave after wave of heated pleasure washed over her. But when he gave her the most intimate kiss a man could give a woman, the sensations threatened to consume her.

"P-please…I can't stand…much more."

He must have realized the depth of her hunger, because he moved to gather her to him, and gazing down at her, tenderly covered her lips with his. His callused palm smoothed over her skin with such infinite care, it brought tears to her eyes and she felt branded by his touch.

Her body trembled with longing as he slid his hand down her side to caress her hip, then her inner thigh. But when he cupped the curls at the apex and his finger dipped into the moist folds to stroke and tease, spirals of sheer ecstasy swirled through her. The feelings were so intense, she couldn't have stopped her body's reaction if her life depended on it.

Arching into his touch, she fought for sanity as waves of excitement flowed through her. "P-please—"

"Does that feel good, sweetheart?" His low whisper close to her ear only added to the sweet tension gripping her.

"I…need…you."

In answer to her broken plea, he spread her thighs with his knee and rose over her. She felt the tip of his strong arousal against her, but instead of joining their bodies, he commanded, "Open your eyes, Fin."

The blaze of need in his dark blue gaze took her breath. He was holding himself in check as he slowly, gently pressed forward to fill her completely. He remained perfectly still for several long seconds and she instinctively knew he was savoring the moment, savoring her.

When he pulled his lower body away from hers, then thrust forward, time stood still. He set a slow, rhythmic pace that built her excitement faster than she'd ever dreamed possible. The heat spiraling throughout her body burned higher and brighter with each stroke and she wrapped her arms around his broad back to keep from being lost.

But all too soon, the delicious tension inside of her let go and wave after wave of fulfillment washed over her. Her moan of satisfaction faded to a helpless whimper as her body relaxed and she slowly drifted back to reality.

Only then did she hear Travis groan, then felt

him shutter as the spasms of his release overtook him. When he buried his face in the side of her neck and collapsed on top of her, Fin tightened her arms around him, holding him to her in an effort to prolong the feeling of oneness she had with this wonderful man.

As his breathing eased and he levered himself up on his elbows, he gently brushed a strand of hair from her cheek. "Are you all right?"

Smiling, she cupped his strong jaw with her palm. "That was, without a doubt, the most incredible experience of my life."

His low chuckle as he rolled to her side and gathered her to him sent a fresh wave of heat coursing through her. "If I have my way, it's just the first of many incredible experiences we're going to have this weekend."

A shiver of delight streaked up her spine. "I'm going to hold you to that, cowboy."

"I'd rather have you hold *me* to *you*," he said, brushing her lips with his. "And while you're holding me, we're going to have another one of those incredible experiences."

She felt his body stir against her thigh and her own body answered with a delicious tightening in the pit of her stomach. Wrapping her arms around his shoulders, she smiled. "I'm holding you against me."

His promising grin caused her heart to race. "Honey, I'm about to amaze both of us."

And to her delight, he did just that.

Holding Fin as she slept, Travis stared at the ceiling above his bed and tried to figure out what was going to become of them. They were treading in an area that could very well spell disaster for all concerned.

If it was just between the two of them, the stakes wouldn't be nearly as high. They could explore what was happening between them and if it didn't work out, they could go their separate ways with a minimum of fuss.

But it wasn't just the two of them. There was Jessie and the baby to think about. Whatever happened between him and Fin affected them as well.

Fin had told him up front that she wasn't good at relationships and he'd told her the truth when he'd said he wasn't looking for one. And he hadn't been.

After his wife died, he'd been sure that he'd never care for another woman the way he had for Lauren. But he was beginning to think that he might have been a little hasty in that assumption.

From the minute he'd laid eyes on Fin, he'd been drawn to her like a bee to honey. And apparently, it had been the same for her with him. Her first visit to the ranch was proof of that. They hadn't been able to keep their hands off of each other. But was great lovemaking enough of a base for a long-term relationship?

The way he saw it, they only had three things in common—Jessie, the baby Fin was carrying and an insatiable need for each other. Other than that, their lives were about as different as night and day.

He was country from his wide-brimmed Resistol hat to the soles of his Justin boots. His life was hard, grueling hours of work spent outside in all kinds of weather, and at night he slept with nothing to listen to but the crickets and an occasional coyote howling off in the distance. And he was much more comfortable in a honky-tonk where the music was loud, the beer was cheap and wearing a new pair of jeans and a clean shirt from the local Wal-Mart was considered dressed up than he'd ever be putting on a suit to go to a Broadway production or some trendy nightclub.

And as foreign as his life was to Fin, her life was just as foreign to him. She lived and worked in a city that never slept. Hell, how could it? With taxis honking and sirens blaring all the time, it was no wonder people were up around the clock. And that was just the tip of the iceberg.

Day in and day out, she worked in a climate-controlled office where the only time she felt the warmth of the sun on her face was when she stood close to the window, and every piece of clothing she owned had some famous designer's name stitched into the label. Even the jeans she'd been wearing at the ranch had some guy's name plastered across the back pocket.

When Fin stirred in her sleep, he tightened his arms around her and pressed a kiss to the top of her head. On her first visit to the Silver Moon, she'd mentioned that she loved the wide open space, but after a while the novelty would wear off and she'd go stir-crazy from missing the hustle and bustle of New York. He had no doubt, he'd be just as unhappy if he had to live in a crowded city.

As he felt sleep finally begin to overtake him, Travis closed his eyes and wondered how they were possibly going to share the raising of a child. Kids needed stability and permanence, not being bounced back and forth between two entirely different worlds.

As he drifted off with no more answers than he'd had before, his dreams were filled with images of sharing his life on the Silver Moon with a green-eyed, auburn-haired woman and child.

Eight

"What do I do first?"

Smiling, Travis handed Fin the keys to the old truck he used for hauling hay. "Put the key in the ignition and your right foot on the brake."

"That's simple enough," she said, doing as he instructed. "What's next?"

Fin's pleased expression caused his chest to tighten. He couldn't get over how excited she was at the prospect of learning to drive and he wouldn't have missed teaching her for anything in the world.

"Turn the key toward the dashboard. When you hear it start, let go of the key."

When the truck's engine fired up, she beamed. "I can't believe I'm actually going to do this."

"I think that's what you said last night when we—"

"You have a one-track mind, cowboy," she interrupted, laughing.

Feeling younger than he had in years, he grinned. "It's incredible, as well as amazing, wouldn't you agree?"

"Your mind or last night?"

"Both."

When she took her foot off the brake, the engine died. "What happened?"

He gave her a kiss that left them both needing resuscitation and when he finally raised his head, she gave him a look that was supposed to be stern, but only made her look more adorable. At least, to him.

"Back to business, cowboy. You're supposed to be teaching me how to drive."

"You have to keep your foot on the brake until you put it in gear or the engine will die."

She frowned. "This is going to start getting complicated, isn't it?"

"Not at all. Before you know it, it'll be second nature to you." He pointed to the ignition. "Put your foot back on the brake, start it up and take hold of the gearshift. Then, without taking your foot off the brake, pull the shift slightly forward and then down until the little indicator on the dash lights up the 'D'."

"Done," she said, looking more confident as she followed his directions.

"You're doing great. Now lightly step on the gas feed." He'd no sooner gotten the words out than she stomped on the gas and the truck shot forward at what seemed like the speed of light.

"This is fun."

"Holy hell!" They spoke at the same time.

It had been ten years since he'd taken Jess out in the same pasture for her first driving lesson, but he remembered it as if it were yesterday. They'd raced across the field and barely missed running off into a small pond.

As the truck bounced across the pasture, Travis tightened his shoulder harness. It seemed that mother and daughter were similar in more ways than just their looks. They both had a foot made of pure lead.

"You might want to take your foot off the front bumper and slow down a little, honey," he said, pulling his hat down tight on his head. He felt like he had in his younger days when he'd ridden broncs in the local rodeo.

When she eased off the gas a bit, Travis breathed

a little easier. The pond had been filled in a few years ago, and even though the pasture was wide open and there was nothing Fin could crash into, he was still glad the horses were safe in their stalls in the barn.

"I should have learned to drive years ago," she said, her cheeks flushed with excitement. "This is a lot more fun than having a driver take me where I want to go."

"I've created a monster," he groaned. His stomach clenched into a tight knot just thinking about her trying to drive in New York City traffic. "You aren't thinking about getting a license and a car, are you?"

"Hardly. There isn't enough room in the city for all the cars now. And parking is an absolute nightmare." She gave him an indulgent look. "I'll limit my driving to the Silver Moon and this pasture."

His heart stalled, then took off at a gallop. She was talking as if she'd be visiting the ranch quite frequently and that pleased him to no end.

"That makes me feel somewhat better," he said when she turned the truck in a tight circle and headed back the way they'd come. As they barreled toward the barn, he decided the horses might not be as safe as he'd first thought. "When you put your foot on the brake, give yourself plenty of room. These things don't stop on a dime."

Apparently, she took him at his word because in the next instant, Fin planted her foot on the brake and the truck skidded to a bone-jarring halt. "I suppose there's a trick to making a smooth stop," she said, frowning.

Reaching over to the steering column, he turned off the key and put the truck in Park. "We'll work on that the next time," he said, thanking the good Lord above for whoever invented antilock brakes.

She surprised him when she unbuckled her shoulder harness, then leaned over and wrapped her arms around his neck. "Thank you, Travis."

"For what?"

"I'm learning all kinds of incredible things this weekend," she said, giving him a smile that sent his temperature skyward.

He grinned as he pulled her close. "Is that so?"

The impish sparkle in her emerald eyes as she nodded fascinated him. "Some of what I learned was particularly amazing."

Lowering his head, he kissed her soundly. "What do you say we go back to the house for a while?"

"Did you have something in mind?" Her whispered words in his ear had him harder than hell in about two seconds flat.

Nodding, he unbuckled the shoulder harness, got out of the truck and walked around the front to slide in behind the steering wheel. "I want to show you something."

She grinned. "Is it incredible?"

He started the truck and, putting it into gear, laughed as he drove toward the house. "Honey, prepare yourself to be downright amazed."

"Have you given any thought to our situation?" Fin asked as she and Travis prepared dinner together. She was supposed to return to New York tomorrow morning and they still hadn't discussed anything about the baby, let alone made a decision.

"A little, but I haven't come to any conclusions," he said, tending to a couple of breaded steaks he was frying in a big cast-iron skillet.

"Me, either." Cutting up vegetables for a garden salad, she thoughtfully nibbled on a sliver of carrot. "I think it's only fair that we have equal time with her."

"Or him." Travis gave her a grin that sent her pulse racing. "There's a fifty percent chance the baby is a boy."

"True."

She turned back to the task at hand before her hormones diverted her attention from the subject. It seemed that with nothing more than a look or a touch, she and Travis gave in to the electrifying passion between them and found themselves in each other's arms.

Slicing a cucumber, she arranged the circles on top of a bed of lettuce. "I don't think we'll have much of a problem with equal time until he or she reaches school age."

He chuckled. "You're ahead of me. I can't think past how I'm going to juggle being in New York for your visits to the obstetrician and here, too." He arranged the steaks on two plates, then spooned milk gravy over the tops. "It gets real busy around here in the spring and summer."

"What's it like here in the spring?"

She loved hearing Travis talk about the ranch. From everything she'd seen and heard, it had to be one of the most tranquil places on earth.

"After the snow melts, everything is green." He smiled. "Then, when the wildflowers start to bloom, there's all kinds of colors mixed in."

"It sounds absolutely beautiful."

He nodded. "With the snowcapped mountains in the distance it looks a lot like the postcards they sell at the tourist places over in Colorado Springs."

"I'd love to see it," she said, unable to keep the wistful tone from her voice.

When he slipped his arms around her waist from behind, she leaned back against his solid frame. "If you'd like, after the baby comes, I'll take you on a trail ride up to some of the upland meadows."

Turning to face him, Fin put her arms around his shoulders, raised up on her tiptoes and kissed his cheek. "I'd love that, Travis. But I still haven't learned to ride a horse."

"And you're not going to until after the baby's born." He shook his head. "I'm not willing to take the chance of you falling. It might cause you to lose the little guy."

It was completely ridiculous, but his statement caused her heart to squeeze painfully. She knew this would be his only biological child, and therefore as important to him as it was to her. But was the baby the only one he was worried about?

It was an undeniable fact that they were extremely attracted to each other physically. That was the reason they found themselves in their current set of circumstances. But was that as far as it went for him? Was the baby the only one he cared for? And why was she suddenly obsessing over it now?

"Honey, are you all right?"

"I'm a little tired." She stepped back from his embrace. "If you don't mind, I think I'll skip dinner and lay down for a nap."

Fin could tell her sudden mood swing confused him, but that couldn't be helped. She needed time to think, time to sort through her feelings and try to understand why it was suddenly so important that the baby wasn't his only concern.

Wanting to get away from him before she did something stupid like burst into tears, she hurried down the hall and started up the stairs. But she suddenly had the strange sensation of flying a moment before she landed in a heap on the hardwood floor.

As she lay there wondering what on earth had happened, a sharp pain knifed through her left side, taking her breath, causing her to draw her legs into a fetal position. Her pulse thundered in her ears and as the room began a sickening spin, she felt herself being drawn into a fathomless black abyss.

She thought she heard Travis call her name, but the beckoning shadows refused to release her. As she gave in to the mist closing around her, her last thought was of losing the baby she wanted so desperately and the man she'd come to love.

Seated in the waiting area at the emergency room, Travis was about two seconds away from tearing the hospital apart if somebody didn't tell him something, and damned quick, about Fin's condition. When he'd brought her in for treatment, they'd run him out of the examining room and he hadn't been allowed back in there since.

He let out a frustrated breath and scrubbed his hands over his face. When he'd heard the loud thump in the living room, followed by an eerie silence, his heart felt as if it had dropped to his boot tops. He'd called her name as he started down the hall to see what happened, but at the sight of her crumpled body lying at the bottom of the stairs the blood in his veins had turned to ice water and he was pretty sure it had taken a good ten years off his life.

"Mr. Clayton?"

When he looked up, a woman in a white lab coat stood at the swinging double doors leading to the treatment area. Jumping to his feet, he walked over to her. "What's going on?"

"I'm Doctor Santos, the on-call OB/GYN," she said, shaking his hand.

"Is Fin going to be all right?" he demanded. If she lost the baby, he'd mourn. But if it came down to her life or the baby's, there was no choice. He wanted the best care humanly possible for Fin.

Smiling, the doctor nodded. "Ms. Elliott cracked a rib when she fell, but I think she and the baby will both be fine. She's healthy and the pregnancy seems to be a normal one, so I don't foresee any problems."

"Thank God." The degree of relief he felt was staggering and his knees wobbled as if they'd turned to rubber.

"She'll need to be on bed rest for the next few days and I wouldn't advise traveling for a couple of weeks. But after that, if she doesn't experience any more problems, she should be able to resume normal activities." The woman scribbled something on the chart she held, then she looked up and her brown-eyed gaze met his. "And it would be best to refrain from sexual intercourse until she goes back for her next prenatal check."

"Can I see her?" he asked, anxious to see with his own eyes that Fin was okay.

"She's getting dressed now," Dr. Santos said, turning to go back through the swinging doors. "You might want to go get your truck and bring it around to the patient pick-up area."

He frowned. "You're sending her home? Shouldn't you keep her for observation or something?"

It wasn't that he didn't want to take Fin back to the ranch. He did. But he wanted the best care possible for her.

"Relax, Mr. Clayton." The woman's dark eyes twinkled. "Believe me, she'll get a lot more rest at home than she would here. And of course, bring her back if she experiences any further problems."

Five minutes later, when he parked outside of the doors designated for discharged patients, a nurse pushed Fin in a wheelchair out to the truck. Once he had her comfortably settled on the bench seat, he slid in behind the steering wheel and started the thirty-mile drive back to the Silver Moon.

"Did the doctor tell you that I'm going to have to extend my stay with you?"

Fin's voice sounded weak and shaky and it just about tore him apart. She was one of the strongest women he'd ever met and it took a lot to bring her down. But he had a feeling that she was shaken more by the thought that she could have lost the baby than from physical pain.

"I wouldn't mind if you wanted to spend the rest of your pregnancy on the Silver Moon," he said, taking her hand in his.

She gave him a tired smile. "That would be nice, but I need to get back to the magazine."

Her words were like a sucker punch to his gut and a definite wake-up call for him. Of course, she'd want to get back to that damned magazine and the contest for CEO of her dad's publishing company. Jess had told him that Fin lived and breathed *Charisma*. She was the first one in the office in the morning and the last one to go home at night.

He'd lost a lot of sleep speculating on whether

anything could ever come of the attraction between them. It looked as if he'd just gotten the answer.

"Ooh. That doesn't feel good at all," Fin said, holding her side as she rose to her feet and took a tentative step toward the dresser. She'd known that moving around was going to hurt, but she hadn't realized how much.

Sitting on the side of Travis's bed for the past several minutes, she'd been trying to work up the courage to walk over and get her purse. She'd needed to call the office and talk to Cade. He was going to have to assume her duties for the next two weeks and keep *Charisma* on track to win Patrick's contest. Even though she had no intention of accepting the position, she wanted to win and prove to Patrick, once and for all, that his daughter wasn't a complete disappointment.

"What the hell do you think you're doing?"

Travis's booming voice made her jump and the movement jarred her sore ribs, causing them to hurt more. "I need my cell phone."

"Why didn't you ask me to get it for you?" Placing the bed tray he carried on top of the dresser, he helped her back to bed. "Is it in your purse?"

"Yes." As she reclined against a mountain of pillows, she took shallow breaths until the ache in her side receded. "I need to call the office and have Cade take over for me until I get back."

He handed her the purse. "Isn't this his and Jessie's first day back from the honeymoon?"

Nodding, she dug around in the bottom of the bag for her cell phone. "What a thing to come home to. He's still basking in the glow of being a newlywed and I'm going to tell him he has to put his nose to the grindstone and not look up until I get back."

Travis chuckled. "Jess might not take too kindly to that, either."

"I can almost guarantee that she'll stay at the office with him." Laughing, she held her side. "Even laughing hurts."

His teasing expression changed immediately. "Are you sure you're all right? No other signs that something else could be wrong?"

"None," she said, shaking her head. She concentrated on the phone in her hand so he wouldn't see the disappointment she felt at his concern for her pregnancy and not her.

She could feel his eyes watching her for several long moments before he finally cleared his throat and hooked his thumb over his shoulder toward the dresser. "I'll take your breakfast back to the kitchen and keep it warm for you. Let me know when you get off the phone and I'll bring it back up."

"Thank you," she mouthed as Chloe answered on the other end of the line.

While her assistant went through the spiel of which office she'd reached and whom she was speaking to, Fin watched Travis glance her way once more as he carried the tray from the room. She could tell he wasn't happy that she was conducting business instead of resting, but he was wisely keeping quiet about it.

"Chloe, it's Fin," she said, interrupting the young woman.

"Where are you? Why aren't you here at the office? Is everything okay?" The rapid-fire questions were typical Chloe.

Smiling, Fin answered, "I decided to take a weekend trip to Colorado."

"Ooh, you went to see Jessie's father, the cowboy, didn't you?"

"Yes." She listened for a moment as Chloe gushed about how handsome Travis was and how thrilled she was to hear about the baby before Fin interrupted. "Is Cade in his office?"

"He and Jessie arrived an hour ago, disappeared into his office and they haven't been seen since." Chloe giggled. "You know how newlyweds are."

Fin winced. She hated having to be the one to break up their bliss, but this was a business call. She needed to speak to him as his boss, not his new mother-in-law.

"Transfer this call to his office."

"When are you coming back, Fin?" There was an excited edge to Chloe's voice and Fin could tell her assistant had something she wanted to share.

"Probably not for a couple of weeks."

Chloe gasped. "You're kidding, right?"

"Unfortunately, no." Pinching the skin over the bridge of her nose, she tried to ward off the tension headache that threatened. "Now, ring Cade's office for me." She'd put just enough firmness in her voice to let Chloe know that the social part of her call was over.

"Cade McMann." From the slight echo, Fin could tell that he was using the speakerphone.

"Cade, it's Fin. I have something I need you to do."

"Do you need me to come down to your office?" he asked.

Fin sighed. "It wouldn't do you any good. I'm in Colorado."

"You're with Dad at the ranch?" Jessie asked excitedly.

"Yes."

"How long have you been there? Are you staying for a while?" Jessie's excitement seemed to be building.

"Three days. And yes, I'll be staying for the next two weeks."

"Two weeks!" Cade's voice forced Fin to hold the phone away from her ear. "With the competition as tight as it is you're not going to be here?"

"First of all, calm down and listen." When it came to *Charisma*, taking charge and getting results were second nature to her. "You'll be acting editor-in-chief until I return at the end of the month, Cade. Don't let anyone slack off on the push to bring profits up. Have Chloe give you a daily report of what she learns from the accounting department. And go over all ad copy with a fine-tooth comb to make sure it's in order before you send it to production."

"Anything else?"

"Call me every day and let me know how we're doing." She paused. "I don't have to tell you how much I want to win this competition."

"No, Fin. You've made it clear from the start how important this is." There was a long pause and she could tell he was trying to figure out how to word his next question.

"What?"

She could almost see him blow out a frustrated breath. "You haven't taken a vacation in years. Why now? Why couldn't it have waited until January after you've won the CEO position?"

"Believe me, I'd be there if I could."

"Fin, what's wrong?" The concern in her daughter's voice touched her as little else could.

"I'm fine, sweetie. Honest." Explaining what had happened and the doctor's advice, she added, "But I'm not so sure about your dad."

"He's hovering, isn't he?" Jessie guessed. "He doesn't like not being in control and when something like this happens, he always makes a big fuss."

"That's an understatement. He's waiting right now for me to get off the phone so that he can bring me breakfast in bed."

"You do realize he's going to drive you nuts?"

Looking up, Fin watched Travis walk into the room with the bed tray laden with every kind of breakfast food imaginable. "He already is, sweetie."

Nine

Travis cautiously watched Fin walk over to the couch and sit down. He'd tried to get her to take another day to lounge around, but she'd pointed out that the doctor had told her to take it easy for a couple of days and it had already been four since her fall. He hadn't liked it, but he'd reluctantly agreed to her being up as long as he was in the same room with her when she got up and started moving around.

She'd given him a look that would have stopped any of her male coworkers dead in their tracks. But it hadn't fazed him one damned bit. She was on his turf now, not some corporate boardroom where she said "jump" and the people around her asked, "How high?"

"Travis, will you please stop watching me like you think I'm going to fall apart at any moment?" She shook her head. "Aside from my ribs being sore, I'm as healthy as one of your horses."

He shrugged. "You don't look like a horse."

"Thank you." She frowned. "I think."

"Miss Fin, would you like for me to fix you somethin' to eat or drink," Spud asked, walking into the room.

"No, but thank you anyway, Mr. Jenkins," Fin answered politely.

"Well, anything you need, you just give me a holler," Spud said, giving her a toothless grin. "I'll see that you get it."

"I appreciate your kindness," she said, smiling.

Travis eyed the old man as he walked back into the kitchen. Fin had charmed his housekeeper's socks off the first time she'd visited the ranch, and when Spud learned she'd be staying with them for a while, he'd been happier than a lone rooster in an overcrowded hen house.

"I think there's something I need after all." She rose to her feet before Travis could get across the room to help her off the couch.

"Where are you going?" He pointed toward the stairs. "If you need something from the bedroom, I'll get it."

Shaking her head, she walked over to the coat tree by the front door. "I'm going outside for a breath of fresh air."

"Do you think that's a good idea?" he asked, following her.

He knew better than to try to talk her out of it. If there was one thing he'd learned when he was married, it was never tell a woman she couldn't do something. It was a surefire way to get a man in hot water faster than he could slap his own ass with both hands.

Holding her jacket for her, then shrugging into his own, he tried a different angle. "The temperature has dropped a good ten degrees since this morning and we've had a few snow flurries. You might get a chill and shivering would probably cause your ribs to hurt."

"Give it up, cowboy. You and Mr. Jenkins won't let me do anything and I'm going stir-crazy." She smiled. "Now are you going to stand here and argue, or are you coming with me?"

Resigned, he reached around her to open the door. "As long as we're going outside, we might as well check on the horses and see that they have hay and plenty of water." At least if they were in the barn, she'd be sheltered from the wind.

Her green eyes twinkled merrily and she looked so damned pretty, he felt a familiar flame ignite in the pit of his belly. "We're returning to the scene of the crime?"

Laughing out loud, he nodded. "Something like that." He didn't tell her, but be hadn't been able to go into the barn one single time since that night and not think about her and their lovemaking.

"How is the colt?" she asked as they walked across the ranch yard.

He didn't even try to stop his wicked grin. "You actually remember there was a colt?"

"You're incorrigible, Mr. Clayton. Of course, I remember the colt. That's the reason we went into the barn that night in the first place." Her smile did strange things to his insides and reminded him that he hadn't been able to make love to her in what seemed like a month of Sundays. "I'll bet he's changed a lot in the past month."

"All babies, no matter what their species, grow faster in their first year than any other time," he said, nodding. Pushing the barn door open, he waited for Fin to step inside. "When Jess was a baby, she grew so fast there were times I could have sworn she changed overnight."

"Unfortunately, the only memory I have of Jessie as an infant was seeing the nun carry a small bundle away," Fin said, walking up to the over-sized stall where he kept the mare and colt. "Patrick gave them strict orders that he didn't even want me knowing whether I'd had a boy or a girl. But one nurse told me I'd had a perfect little girl before she left the delivery room with Jessie."

Travis's chest tightened at the thought of Fin having to watch her baby being taken away, of never knowing whether she would see her little girl again. "You'll get to watch this baby grow up from the moment he's born, Fin." Slipping his arms around her, he held her close. "We both will."

Nodding, she remained silent and he figured she was struggling to hold her emotions in check.

It just about tore him apart to think of anything causing her such emotional pain and he knew right then and there that he wanted to spend the rest of his life making sure that she never knew another sad moment.

He took a deep breath, then another as the realization spread throughout every fiber of his being. There was no more doubt and no more denial. Whether they came from two different worlds or not, he'd fallen in love with Fin.

It scared the living hell out of him to think that

she might not feel the same. But he knew beyond a shadow of doubt that he had to lay his heart on the line and take that chance. Whether they lived on the Silver Moon or in New York, Fin and the baby were more important to him than taking his next breath. And he had every intention of telling her so.

Lowering his mouth to hers, he gave her a kiss that threatened to buckle his knees and had them both breathing heavily by the time he raised his head. Then, releasing her, he took a step back to keep from reaching for her again.

"As soon as I finish feeding the horses, we're going back to the house for a long talk, sweetheart."

"Cade, are you sure about this?" Fin asked, pacing the length of the living room. "*Charisma* is tied in the competition with *The Buzz*?"

When she and Travis returned from the barn, Spud had informed her that her cell phone had, as he put it, "chirped like a cricket with four back legs" about every five minutes since she'd walked out the door. After checking the caller ID, she'd immediately phoned the office to find out what was so important that Cade had called her four times in less than thirty minutes.

"Chloe heard it first when she was on break this morning. Then Jessie overheard someone from accounting talking about it in the hall." Cade paused. "I'm trying to get the official word on it, but from all indications we've made up the difference and we're in a dead heat with Shane and *The Buzz*."

The information should have excited her beyond words. But as Cade's news sunk in, she found that, although she was proud that it looked as if the hard work she and her team had put into making *Charisma* number one was paying off, it wasn't nearly as important to her as it would have been three weeks ago.

"As soon as you get the information confirmed one way or the other, I want you to call me." She glanced at Travis, standing ramrod straight across the room. He was watching her closely, his expression guarded. "I have to go now. Give Jessie my love."

When she closed the phone and set it on the end table by the couch, Travis nodded. "I take it that your magazine is doing well in your father's competition?"

"At this point, we're holding our own," she said, nodding. "With a little more work, I have no doubt that we'll pull ahead and win."

She watched his broad chest expand as he drew in a deep breath. "Then you'll take over as CEO of your dad's company in January?"

"That's the way Patrick has it set up," she said,

careful to be as noncommittal as possible. She hadn't told anyone that, in the event she won the competition, she'd step down in order to spend as much time as possible with her child.

Travis shook his head. "You didn't answer my question."

Should she tell him that it was no longer as important to her as it had once been? Should she admit that her priorities had changed and she wanted nothing more than to be his wife and their baby's mother?

"I...that is...we—"

She snapped her mouth shut as she struggled to find an answer. It wasn't in her nature to lie. But she wasn't certain she was brave enough to tell him the truth, either.

Would he believe her if she admitted that she'd only used *Charisma* all these years as a substitute for the family she really wanted? How could she put into words, without risking the humiliation of a rejection and a broken heart, how she felt about him? What if he wanted the baby, but not her? What would happen if she told him she'd fallen hopelessly in love with him and wanted to abandon her cold, lonely apartment overlooking Central Park to live with him and their child on the Silver Moon Ranch? Could she survive if he didn't feel the same?

He took a step toward her. "Fin?"

She gave herself a mental shake. What was wrong with her? She was Fin Elliott, a fearless executive who could face any challenge set before her and come out the victor. Why was it so hard for her to find the courage to tell the man of her dreams how she felt and what she wanted?

As she stared into his incredible blue eyes, she knew exactly why she was finding it difficult to express herself. Travis was far more important to her than *Charisma* or the CEO position at EPH had ever been or ever would be.

But when she opened her mouth to tell him so, Travis shook his head. "Before you say a word, I have something to tell you."

"I have something to say to you, too," she said, wishing that he would take her in his arms and give her the slightest indication they were in the same place emotionally.

"You can have your say, after I've had mine." He pointed to the couch. "You might want to sit down. I'm not very good at stuff like this and it could take awhile."

Lowering herself to the leather couch, she held her breath as she waited for him to tell her what was so important to him.

"When Jessie first talked about trying to find you, I was dead set against it."

Fin felt certain that her heart shattered into a million pieces and she wasn't entirely sure that she'd be able to draw her next breath for the devastating emotion tightening her chest. "I…didn't know. Jessie never said how you felt about our meeting."

"I was dead wrong and she was right not to tell you." He rubbed the back of his neck as if to ease tension. "You've got to understand, Fin. I wasn't sure you'd be all that receptive to meeting a daughter you gave up for adoption all those years ago. You were extremely young and some women want to forget something like that ever happened to them." He gave her an unapologetic look. "And from the minute my wife and I adopted Jessie, I dedicated my life to protecting her from anything that would harm her physically or emotionally."

Fin swallowed hard. Jessie couldn't have been placed with a better family than the Claytons. And although it had been the hardest thing Fin had ever had to do, Jessie had fared far better having Travis for her father than she would have with Fin raising her alone.

She could understand his reasoning, but it still hurt to think that if Jessie had listened to him, they might never have met. "You were afraid I'd reject her," Fin whispered brokenly.

He nodded. "I spent many a sleepless night

before Jess called to tell me how happy you'd been when she finally told you who she was."

Tears filled Fin's eyes. "I loved and wanted her from the moment I discovered I was pregnant."

"I know that now." He smiled. "In fact, the first time I laid eyes on you, I knew you were nothing like what I'd feared you would be."

"Really?" she asked cautiously.

He sat down on the raised stone hearth in front of her. "Instead of a corporate executive with a killer instinct, you were warm, personable and sexier than sin."

She almost choked. She'd never associated herself with the word sexy. "Me?"

"Honey, you've had me turned wrong side out ever since I first laid eyes on you."

His laughter warmed her, but she tried not to let her hopes build. Sexual attraction was one thing, but he hadn't mentioned anything about loving her.

"I don't think there's ever been a doubt for either of us that we share an irresistible chemistry," she said, nodding.

"But we've had some huge problems from the get-go," he said, his expression turning serious. "You live in New York and my life is out here in God's country. Your career is glamorous and impressive as hell." He shrugged his wide shoulders. "I'm nothing more than a rancher, leading a simple, uncomplicated life. I couldn't see anything coming of the attraction between us."

Her heart sank. Was he trying to tell her all the reasons that a relationship between them wouldn't work? That he wasn't even willing to give them a fair chance?

His gaze dropped to his loosely clasped hands hanging between his knees. "Then we put the cart before the horse. We discovered that I'd gotten you pregnant before we'd even really gotten to know each other."

She swiped at an errant tear as it slid down her cheek. "You see our baby as a problem?"

"Hell no." There was no hesitation in his adamant answer. "I couldn't be happier about our having a child together." He stood up and walked over to where she sat on the couch. "But what I'm not happy about is trying to juggle time and distance in the raising of him."

"Or her."

"Right." He dropped down to one knee and took her hands in his. "I've never done anything half-assed in my entire life and I'm not about to start now. I don't want to be a part-time dad any more than you want to be a part-time mother."

Her heart skipped several beats. "What are you saying, Travis?"

"I want us to get married, Fin," he said seriously. "I want both of us to be full-time parents and raise this baby together."

He'd talked about wanting their baby and his desire to be with the child, but he hadn't mentioned anything about loving and wanting her. "I...don't know what to say."

He leaned forward and gently pressed his lips to hers. "'Yes' would work for me, honey."

She had to clear her suddenly dry throat before she could get her vocal cords to work. Being Travis's wife was what she wanted more than anything, but not without his love.

Touching his cheek, she shook her head. "Unfortunately, it doesn't work for me."

Ten

Travis felt like a damned fool. He'd laid his heart, as well as his pride, on the line and Fin had just the same as stomped all over them.

Releasing her hand, he took a deep breath and stood up. In all of his forty-nine years, he'd never dreamed that he could hurt so much and not have something physically wrong. Gathering what was left of his dignity, he squared his shoulders and met her gaze head-on.

"Well, I guess all there is left to do now is figure out who gets the baby on holidays and where he—"

"Or she."

He nodded. "Or she will spend the summers."

Suddenly needing to put distance between them, he turned toward the door. "Let me know whatever you think is fair and I'll go along with it."

"Hold it right there, cowboy." Fin's hand on his arm stopped him cold.

Her touch burned right through his shirt and the pain in his chest tightened unbearably. Glancing down at her soft palm on his arm, then back at her beautiful face, he wanted nothing more than to take her in his arms and try to convince her that they belonged together. But he'd never begged for anything in his life and, God help him, he'd never been tempted to do so—until now.

"You've had your say, now I'm going to have mine." Her green eyes sparkled with determination and he loved her more in that moment than life itself.

"What do you want from me, Fin? I offered marriage and you turned me down."

"That's just it." She rose to her feet, then pushing him down on the couch, she planted her fists on her slender hips as she glared down at him. "You didn't ask me to marry you. You offered."

Damn, but she was gorgeous when she pitched a hissy fit. But as her words sank in, he frowned. "It's the same thing."

"No, it's not." She started pacing. "There's a big difference. Huge even."

He noticed that Spud had walked in to see what all the commotion was about. But one quelling look from the incensed female giving Travis hell had the old geezer retreating back to the safety of the kitchen as fast as his seventy-plus years and arthritis would allow.

"Did it ever occur to you that I might want a marriage proposal that sounded more personal and less like a business merger?"

He frowned. "I didn't mean for it to sound like—"

She held up her hand. "Save it. I'm not finished." Looking every bit as commanding as he knew she had to be in the boardroom, she narrowed her pretty green eyes. "It's all or nothing with me, cowboy. I want it all. Marriage, a cozy home and this baby. And maybe one or two more."

The tightness in his chest eased a bit. "I can give you all of that."

"Yes, you can." Pausing, her voice softened. "But can you give me what I need most of all?"

The tears in her eyes caused a tight knot to form in the pit of his stomach. He couldn't bear to think he'd caused her to cry.

Rising to his feet, he walked over and took her

in his arms. "What do you want, sweetheart? Name it and it's yours."

"I want you to want me, as well as the baby. I want to be your wife. I want to share your life here on the Silver Moon." Her voice dropped to a broken whisper. "I want…your love, Travis."

If he could have managed it, he would have kicked his own tail end. He might have been proposing marriage, but he hadn't bothered to tell Fin how much she'd come to mean to him, how he loved her and needed her more than he needed his next breath.

Holding her close, he lowered his mouth to hers and gave her a kiss filled with the promise of a lifetime of everything she wanted. "I'm sorry, honey. I told you I wasn't good at this stuff." Using his index finger to tip her chin up until their gazes met, he smiled. "I love you more than you'll ever know. I have since the minute I first saw you."

"Oh, Travis, I love you, too. So very much." Wrapping her arms around his waist, she laid her head against his chest. "I was afraid you wanted the baby, but not me."

He kissed her silky auburn hair. "I never again want you to doubt that I want and love you. You own my heart, Fin Elliott. The baby is an extension of that love." Leaning back, he smiled. "Even though

I don't deserve you, will you do me the honor of being my wife, Fin?"

"That's more like it, cowboy." She gave him a watery grin. "Yes, I'll be your wife."

He felt like the luckiest man alive. "I promise to spend the rest of my life making sure you don't regret it, sweetheart. But are you sure you want to live here on the ranch? What about your career? Your apartment in New York? Won't you miss them?"

"No." She placed her soft palm along his jaw and gazed up at him with so much love in her eyes it stole his breath. "When I was a child, my dream in life was to have a husband and family. But after Jessie was taken from me, I made *Charisma* my baby. I nurtured it and watched it grow. But it's time to let my 'baby' go. I've raised her to be a strong force in the fashion industry. Now it's time for me to step back and let someone else guide her while I devote myself to my first dream."

"You won't miss New York?" he asked, still unable to believe that she wanted to give up life as she knew it to marry him and raise their child under the wide Colorado sky.

She shook her head. "I belong here with you on this beautiful ranch." Her smile caused him to go weak in the knees. "I want to raise our children here in this wonderful place. I want to make love with you every night in that big bed upstairs. And I want to sit with you on the swing on the front porch and watch our grandchildren playing in the yard."

He would have told her that he wanted all those things, too, but he couldn't have forced words past the lump in his throat if his life depended on it. Instead, he showed her by placing his lips on hers and kissing her with all the emotion he couldn't put into words.

When he finally raised his head, he smiled. "Who do you think your dad will appoint as editor-in-chief at *Charisma*?"

"I'm not sure." She grinned. "But he'd better do it soon because other than occasional visits to see Jessie and Cade and the rest of the family, I'm not going back."

"How do you think your dad will take the news?"

Fin nibbled on her lower lip as she thought about her father. She'd held a grudge against him all these years, but it truly had been a waste of spirit and energy. It hadn't brought her baby girl back to her. Only time had taken care of that. And if she were perfectly honest with herself, she wouldn't have met the love of her life and had a second chance at motherhood if Patrick hadn't insisted that she give Jessie up for Travis and his wife to adopt.

"Why don't you give him a call?" Travis asked, as if reading her mind.

She sighed. "I'm not sure what to say."

"Start by saying hello." He led her over to the phone. "The rest will take care of itself."

As she dialed her parents at The Tides, Travis disappeared into the kitchen and she knew he was giving her the privacy he thought she needed for the difficult phone conversation. She loved him for it, but he needn't have bothered. She didn't intend for there to be any secrets between them.

"Hi, Mom." Fortunately, instead of the maid answering the phone, her mother had picked up on the second ring.

"Finny, 'tis good to hear your voice." The sound of her mother's Irish lilt caused Fin to smile. Maeve had always been the glue that held the Elliott clan together, despite their share of problems.

"It's good to hear you, too." After exchanging a few inconsequential pleasantries, Fin asked, "Is Patrick home from the office?"

"Yes, dear. He returned from the city about an hour ago."

Fin closed her eyes as she gathered her courage. "Could I speak with him, please?"

When her mother handed the phone to Patrick, his booming voice filtered into her ear. "Hello, Finola."

Taking a deep breath, she forced herself to bring up the subject that had driven them apart over twenty years ago. "I want you to tell me the truth, Patrick. Have you ever regretted forcing me into giving Jessie up for adoption?"

His sharp intake of breath was the only sound she heard from him for several long, nerve-wracking seconds. When he finally spoke, there was a gruffness in his voice that she'd never heard. "I thought I was doing what was best for you at the time, Finola. But in hindsight, it was quite possibly the worst decision I've ever made."

Patrick's admission that he'd been wrong was the last thing she'd expected him to say. "You never told me."

There was a short pause before he spoke again. "I never knew how to tell you how sorry I was that I put my pride and concern for social appearances ahead of your happiness."

"In all fairness, I don't think I ever gave you the chance," Fin said, admitting her own part in the rift.

"I'm—" he stopped to clear his throat "—glad that we've finally got this out in the open, lass."

His use of the pet name he'd called her when she was a little girl caused tears to pool in the corners of her eyes. "I am, too, Dad."

"I...love you, Fin. Can you ever find it in your

heart to forgive me?" The hitch in her father's voice sent tears streaming down her cheeks.

"Yes, Dad. I forgive you."

There was a long pause as if they both needed time to get used to the fact that they'd finally made their peace with the past.

"I'm going to marry Jessie's adoptive father," Fin said, breaking the silence.

"Does he make you happy, lass?" Patrick's voice held a fatherly concern that she knew for certain she'd never heard before.

"Yes, Dad. He makes me very happy."

"I'm glad you found him. He seems like a good, hard-working man. And he did a wonderful job raising Jessica." Her father surprised her further when he added, "I also think it's wonderful that we'll have a new grandchild soon."

"You don't know how much that means to me, Dad," she said, meaning it.

"How are you going to juggle time at the office with a new baby?" he asked, giving her the perfect opportunity to tell him the second reason she'd called.

"I'm not even going to try." She took a deep breath as she prepared to end her career and kiss the CEO position goodbye once and for all. "Effective

immediately I'm no longer the editor-in-chief of
Charisma."

"Are you sure that's what you want?" From the
tone of his voice, she could tell her father already
knew the answer.

"Yes, Dad. I want what Mom always had—time
to be with her babies."

"I can't fault you for that, lass."

"Dad, there's one more thing."

"What's that?"

"I think Cade McMann would be an excellent
candidate for my position. He knows the magazine
inside out and he has fantastic instincts. You can trust
him and his judgment to keep *Charisma* on the right
track."

"And he's part of the family now," her father said,
sounding thoughtful.

After telling her parents again that she loved
them and that she'd see them at the New Year's Eve
party they were holding at The Tides, she hung up
the phone and went in search of Travis. She felt
more at peace than she had in twenty-three years
and finally ready to start the rest of her life.

"You look absolutely beautiful, Fin."

Smiling at her daughter, Fin asked, "Is your dad
ready?"

"I think he's going to wear a hole in the floor from pacing so much," Jessie said, laughing as she finished with the tiny buttons at the back of Fin's wedding dress. "Cade and Mac have both threatened to tie him down and Spud offered to supply the rope."

Fin laughed. "He asked me two days ago if we couldn't just elope."

Tears filled Jessie's eyes as she nodded. "Dad loves you so much. We all do."

"And I love all of you." Fin gave her daughter a watery smile. "Here we go again. We're both going to ruin our makeup if we don't stop crying."

Dabbing at her eyes with a tissue, Jessie smiled. "I'm just so happy for both of you."

Fin hugged Jessie close. "I'm happy for all of us. I have a beautiful daughter, a wonderful son-in-law and I'm marrying the man I love."

"It's time, Aunt Finny."

Looking up, Fin smiled at her niece. Marriage to Mac Riggs definitely agreed with Bridget. There was a sparkle in her eyes and a glow about her that hadn't been there before she met the tall, dark-haired sheriff of Winchester County.

"We'll be right there," Jessie said, hugging Fin again. "Let's go take pity on Dad before he has to have the floor resurfaced."